Rat

A Cop's Secret Weapon

Edmond Gagnon

Rat

A Cop's Secret Weapon

Dedication

for

Jesse William Trudell
1983 – 2006

Jesse passed well before his time
and could not follow in his father's footsteps,
fulfilling his dream
of becoming a police officer.

Edmond Gagnon

1
Crazy Jerry

"All that is necessary for the triumph of evil is for good men to do nothing."

- Edmund Kist

On June 1st, 1979, Norm Strom was promoted to the rank of Constable on the city police force. That title meant he'd be wearing a police uniform that included hand cuffs, a night stick, and a gun. He had been a police cadet for the two years prior, handing out parking tickets and serving summonses and subpoenas.

The promotion meant he'd be a real cop, assigned to walking a beat downtown. Back then, the downtown core was divided into four walking beats, with one man on foot in each area. The city itself is located at the bottom end of Canada; some folks referred to it as the asshole of Canada because of its location.

Norm was actually born in a small town, just outside the city he grew up in. He worked from the age of twelve doing a couple different paper routes and cleaning up at construction sites. In his later teens, he put up aluminum siding until he landed a full-time warehouse job.

Norm was left to be the man of the house when he was eleven, after his parents divorced, leaving his mother with six children. He was the eldest and had the responsibility of looking after his siblings, while his mother tried to hold down three different jobs. It was his upbringing that forged his character, especially his fortitude and leadership abilities.

Norm was an all-star jock in high school, but he found that he would have to work for a living to get what he wanted from life. His mother had no time to be a soccer mom, driving her kids all over the city. Norm learned to be independent and self sufficient. He was a big guy, but easy going and an attractive candidate for the police force. Long hair was in style back then, so Norm had to get a standard cop hair cut. It highlighted his baby face, making him look like he was twelve years old again. He was hired by the city police force a month before his nineteenth birthday.

The city was considered blue collar and a lunch bucket town. The automotive industry basically supported the city and employed most of Norm's buddies. Granted, the city changed dramatically over the last thirty-something years. It lays directly across the border from a gritty metropolis in the United States. The border city is a gateway to Canada, where tens of thousands of vehicles per day enter the country. Most pass through, but many stay and play.

The makeup of the downtown area was much different in the days that Norm walked the beat, there were dozens of shops and boutiques with a few large stores like Kresge and Woolworth. The sidewalks were bustling with people during the day, but deserted at night. There were no all-night coffee shops, only one small diner that stayed open until 3:00am. After that, there were really only the cops on the beat, and criminals on the street. Police portable radios were something new at the time. There were no pagers, cell phones, or other mobile devices. It was a cold and lonely job at 4:00am in the dead of winter.

Walking a beat was pretty mundane and uneventful, but you got plenty of exercise being on your feet for eight hours. That was what Norm's training officer Andy Green had told him on his first day as he tried to keep up to Andy's much longer stride. The training period lasted only two days. Andy was tall, dark, and handsome. He could have been a poster boy for police recruiting. He even had a perfect cop moustache.

Andy taught Norm how to stroll, and look for anything that was out of the ordinary. There was no way that Norm could learn to consume the amount of coffee that Andy did in one day, especially since he hated the stuff. Go figure, a cop who didn't like coffee. Donuts were good though.

Welcome to the Real World

His second day on the beat started the same as the first, but then something happened. The dispatcher called for every available unit to attend the east side of the city, where two small airplanes had collided in mid-air. Norm felt his heart starting to race when one of the patrol cars pulled up to the curb and the driver told him and Andy to jump in.

It was Norm's first lights and siren experience. The police force had just gotten new patrol cars with fancy roof lights and sirens. The old cars had the single cherry on top and a wind-up siren. The ride to the crash scene was a blur. The driver never stopped for any red lights. The siren was ear piercing. He hung on to the seat in front of him and the arm rest beside him. He looked over at Andy to see how he should be acting. Andy just smiled.

The scene of the crash was in complete chaos. More speeding police cars arrived after the one Norm was in. People were crying, screaming, and running all over the place. A neighbor approached Norm carrying a piece of one of the airplanes that had fallen into his back yard. He didn't have a clue as to what he was supposed to do, so he just shadowed Andy. Luckily, the bulk of the wreckage from the two planes landed in an empty field. The crash site was smack dab in the middle of a residential neighborhood.

Norm noticed that there was still some smoke coming from the fuselage of one of the planes. It didn't resemble an airplane in any way, the wings and tail were missing. The metal shell was torn, mangled, and charred from fire. Norm smelled burnt fuel and something else unfamiliar to him when he got closer to the wreck, it was burnt human flesh. He saw the charred remains of the passengers in the plane, there were no survivors.

Norm watched in amazement as a grizzly bear of a man tore through the metal plane with his bare hands to get at the bodies. He was Ted Masterson, the one-man body removal service. It was a horrific scene, Norm's welcome to the ugly side of police work.

Police work consisted of putting in time at the scene, and then putting in time doing the paperwork. In many cases, street cops like Norm never saw the conclusion of any particular case. Follow-up and arrests were made by detectives, and cases could take several months to go to court. As in the case of the plane crash, he read the explanation of the event in the local newspaper the next day. He found that he was part of a team, and that everyone on the team had a specific job to do.

A Little Help from a Friend

As a normie new guy, you were expected to put your time in walking a beat. As you gained seniority and new rookies were hired on, you moved up the chain and eventually into patrol cars. Like the other rookies before him, Norm put in his time. He learned the basics of policing and who the bad guys on his beat were.

He tried to get to know some of the local business owners, proudly patrolling their neighborhood on foot. Norm always smiled and waved as he strolled his beat. Back then, people actually smiled and waved back at you. There was one day in particular where everyone was smiling at Norm, even before he made eye contact with them. He found out why later. He removed his hat at lunch and saw that a pigeon had shit all over the top of it.

Norm got a call from his old neighborhood friend Jerry one day, he said he had some information for him. He had known Jerry for a few years before becoming a cop. He was a good guy, but not quite your model citizen. Gerald was his proper name, but he was known as Crazy Jerry on the street. He had some minor brushes with the law, but he was never arrested or charged with anything criminal. He was the guy in the hood to go to if you needed anything.

Jerry knew people, who knew people, who could get you drugs, car and motorcycle parts, or even decoy ducks. Once, Jerry went to *borrow* some decoys from somebody's basement storage area and he found three pounds of pot instead. Jerry, Norm, and all their buddies were high for days. He came to realize that his circle of friends had to change when he became a cop. He had to quit smoking up with the boys and stop hanging out with Jerry.

Jerry said he had some information that would earn Norm some Brownie points at work. He made it quite clear that he wasn't a rat and that he just wanted to help Norm with his career. Norm already knew that a rat was someone who supplied information to the police. What he didn't know was how they would later help to influence his police career.

Jerry said that he had been in a bar, and that he overheard some guys talking about a heist they had pulled. The guys were talking about a tool and die shop they had broken into. They did the B & E, stole the company truck, and then filled it with stolen tools. Jerry gave Norm a pretty vague description of the guys, but he was sharp enough to copy down the license plate number of their truck.

Norm wasn't quite sure what to do with Jerry's information, so he asked a senior guy for advice on how to write up the report. He was taught how to keep Jerry's name out of the report, referring to him only as a confidential source. Jerry had just become Norm's first informant.

He submitted his report to the detectives and they issued a bulletin with the details that he had supplied them. The bulletin included the business that had in fact, been broken into. Norm blushed when his Sergeant read out the bulletin, but he also felt a sense of pride. Every day during roll call, patrol officers receive several bulletins prior to the start of their shift.

Norm went about his business that day, walking his beat as usual, when he spotted a truck bearing the same license plates as the one that he had reported. What were the chances of that? He should have bought a lottery ticket that same day. Norm called the detectives and they told him to keep an eye on the truck until they got there.

The detectives arrested the Duchene brothers when they returned to their truck. Some of the stolen tools were found in the truck and the detectives got a search warrant for the Duchene house. They arrested a third dirt bag there. Norm and the detectives recovered over ten thousand dollars in stolen tools from the house. All three men were charged with the B & E and possession of stolen property.

Norm cherished the fact that the detectives included him in the search of the house and the arrest, giving him credit for the bust. He was the rookie though and had to do the dirty work, crawling through the dark and filthy crawl space. The veteran detectives were Gods to a rookie like Norm, who was at the bottom of the totem pole. They submitted a report to his commander and he received a divisional commendation for his devotion and dedication to duty. Norm scored some Brownie points thanks to Jerry.

Libation and Celebration

The least Norm could do to thank Jerry was to buy him a few drinks. The outing started in the city on Jerry's turf, but Norm thought he'd give his old buddy a glimpse of his new world and his new buddies in blue. There was a particular bar in the U.S. that cops from both sides of the border hung out at. When they let their hair down, they want to be among their own, someone they can trust when their backs are turned.

If you've ever noticed an off-duty cop in a public place, he will usually have his back to the wall with his eyes continuously scanning the room. They are trained to be aware of their surroundings at all times and to be prepared for any situation that might present itself.

On that particular night, Jerry was in for a treat. He got a few stares from some of the boys, but Norm gave them the nod to acknowledge Jerry was with him. Close friends were accepted as well as groupies or girlfriends. Wives were *not* allowed. There were only a handful of women on the job back then, so the room was full of cock and balls. You could pretty well smell the testosterone in the air.

There were more guys than usual in the bar, apparently one of them was having a makeshift bachelor party. Jerry and Norm were working on their first beer when someone at the bar pointed up to the man of the hour. It was the future groom, Manny in all his glory. He was standing on the bar with his pants down around his ankles. Egged on by his buddies, Manny attempted to belly dance while someone tried to stuff a pickled egg into his navel.

Norm didn't know Manny that well. He was known as Mad Manny. The word was that the name came from his high school football days. He definitely had the build of a football player, and was louder than any sports announcer. The guys said he ran like a deer and was a good street cop. Whether it was a police uniform, or an expensive suit, Manny always looked like he had just slept in it. His true claim to fame was that he could stuff a whole Big Mac into his mouth without chewing it. Apparently, he had once attempted a Whopper, but it started to come out his nose and he almost choked to death.

Jerry nudged Norm with his elbow as Manny posed on the corner of the bar. He was looking up at the ceiling and before anyone could catch on to what was about to happen, Manny leaped up and grabbed the chandelier. He crashed down on top of the pool table to the cheers and laughter of the crowd. Without missing a beat, one of the guys playing pool tried to bank the cue ball off Mad Manny's bare ass.

The bar owner, who was usually pretty tolerant of his drunken cop patrons, was not impressed. He suggested it was time to take Manny home. Norm told Jerry to drink up while he went to find their ride home. They had caught a lift with Frankie on the way there. Norm had last seen him at the pinball machine where a groupie chick was working the game's flippers and Frankie was reaching around from behind her, working her titties. Norm couldn't find him anywhere in the bar. Someone said to try Lola's place out back.

Lola was a big black hooker who serviced some of the guys when they needed to relieve a little stress. She lived directly behind the bar. Norm made his way through the poker game in the back room on the way to Lola's place. One of the guys had just thrown his pay check into the pot. He found Frankie at Lola's, but he was preoccupied. His pants were down around his ankles and he was banging Lola from behind. Lola, in turn, was blowing one of the other guys. It was a tag team event. The threesome looked like an Oreo cookie in reverse. Norm's naivety was fading fast, with his new discoveries on and off the job.

Dogs and Guns

Jerry and Norm caught a ride with some other guys to grab a Coney dog on the way home. The Coney Island at 3:30 in the morning was always entertaining. Mad Manny was already there, wearing one of the waiter's aprons and taking orders. The place was packed with drunks and very loud. Then Manny said the word *nigger* purposely loud enough for everyone, including the only black man in the place, to hear it. The pure silence that followed made the room stand still. The black man stood up and pulled out a huge silver gun and pointed it directly at Manny.

Only the black guy and Mad Manny remained standing, everyone else had hit the floor except for Marty James. He casually positioned himself between the two men and then softly explained to the black man with the big silver gun what Manny had actually said was *Pigger*. That just happened to be the nick name of one of the other guys. It had to be the only acceptable explanation that the black man wanted to hear, because he didn't pull the trigger. The poor bastard probably realized he'd never make it out of there alive if he had shot Mad Manny.

Marty James could have been a hostage negotiator, but he was too much of a rebel. He could have been a company man, but his attitude changed years earlier after he shot a guy who charged at him wielding a hammer. It was one of those split-second decisions that didn't play out well in the media, and Marty was made out to be the bad guy. It's always easier to judge when you're not the one being attacked.

The police brass never did anything to back up Marty's decision. It was like they thought he should have taken a whack on the head before he shot the guy. Marty was left with a bad taste in his mouth; he lost his motivation and respect for the rules of the job. He grew his hair and moustache beyond regulation, and he only worked to rule. He answered his calls for service, but never went out of his way to write any tickets. Rebels were often looked up to within the ranks, it must have had something to do with the bad boy image.

To add to his God-like status, Marty managed one more feat the night of Mad Manny's party. Norm went to take a piss before heading home and bumped into two other cops who were peaking through a hole in the men's bathroom door. They told Norm that Marty had announced a *fugly* contest earlier in the evening. That's where you pick the ugliest women in the place and try to have sex with her. Marty claimed his prize and he was banging her on the sink in the men's room.

Sadly, Marty James died a few years later. His heavy drinking caught up to him one night when a hydro pole jumped out in front of him on his way home. Even in death, Marty was chastised by the media. Norm will never forget listening to the two veteran cops who got the accident call. They didn't recognize the dead man until they rolled him over. His badge fell out of his pocket and on to the road, it was Marty James.

Gerry and Norm had their fill of beer and Coney dogs and decided it was time to head home. Somehow, there were now more passengers than there were cars. Someone had obviously taken off, leaving the others behind. Seven guys packed into a compact car. There were three in the front, and four in the back. There were still two guys who refused to be left behind, and they climbed into the trunk. Apparently the second guy couldn't wedge himself into the trunk, so he decided to ride on the roof. Norm, the new guy, was told do drive the stick shift that he was not familiar with.

"No problem," Jerry said.

"You work the pedals, and I'll do the shifting."

It all seemed like fun and games until the car pulled up to the Customs booth on the Canadian side of the border. The guy on the roof was wailing, pretending he was a police siren. The poor border guard just pretended that he didn't see anything and waved the car through.

Norm was somewhat amazed that Jerry hadn't said much all night, although he seemed to be thoroughly enjoying himself.

It wasn't until Norm dropped him off that Jerry said, "Your cop buddies are fucking crazy, worse than my biker buddies."

In all honesty, Norm had begun to wonder himself, exactly what he had gotten into.

It wasn't just a job; it was a fucking adventure.

2
The Rookie

"Courage, above all things, is the first quality of a warrior."
- Karl Von Clausewitz

What exactly is a cop and where does the word come from? Norm asked himself and others that question. Answers and definitions varied. Nobody seemed to be really sure as to where the word came from. Some said it was short for *copper*, derived from the old copper buttons police wore on their uniforms, and others said police originally wore copper badges. Other definitions were: *constable on patrol* or *citizen on patrol*. It seemed everyone had their own definition.

Research the word on the Internet and Snopes refers to two different sources: The Chambers Dictionary of Etymology and The Encyclopedia of Word and Phrase Origins.

According to these sources, the word *cop* evolved from 1844 to 1859 when *cop* meant to take or seize. Thus, *coppers* were those who would *take into police custody*. The word cop has stuck with the police ever since. A century later more colorful names like fuzz and pig were added to the list.

Normie New Guy

Even though Norm was promoted to constable, he was still considered a rookie by all those who were senior to him. This not only meant he'd be doing the lowest job on the totem pole, but that he'd also be doing just about anything else that was asked of him by his seniors. This meant coffee runs for the boss and shuffling police cars around in the parking lot for the guys who actually got to drive them. He learned other jobs like relieving the station man or cell man when they went for lunch. This was a great learning experience at times, but Norm felt like a yo-yo, being called in and out of the station from his walking beat.

One of the jobs he hated the most was traffic direction. When a particular intersection got backed up or there was a car accident, he was sent to clear up the mess. That is when Norm learned how stupid some drivers really are, he had to have eyes in the back of his head so he didn't get run over. He found it especially fun having to direct traffic in the pouring rain without any rain gear. It was the job, and you had to stay put until the sergeant said you could leave.

At times, Norm was completely forgotten about, he'd have to call the dispatcher to be relieved. Standing in freezing rain with your bladder about to explode, was not fun. Then every once in a while, someone senior would feel the need to break the rookie in and have him do something stupid, like attending all the offices in the building asking for a left-handed stapler.

Being a rookie full of piss and vinegar, he chomped at the bit hoping to get into some real action. Occasionally a patrol car on the way to a fight would come screeching up to the curb telling Norm to get in. He'd get all worked up racing to the call, only to find the fight was over by the time that they got there.

Norm was to discover what was a cop's real job—cleaning up the mess, sorting it all out, writing down all the pertinent information, and looking after the victims. He also learned that cops could become victims too.

While walking the beat one evening, he heard a dispatch over the radio that puts a knot in every cop's stomach.

"Officer needs assistance."

The call was from an off-duty cop who was working a huge bash at the university. The city allowed the police to work off-duty at some bars which in effect, reduced calls for service to those particular establishments. The cops working off-duty got paid for the job by the owner of the business. Norm worked some of those jobs, it was a great way to make some extra cash and meet chicks.

He felt helpless as patrol cars replied to the dispatcher that they were responding to the call. Just as he was feeling completely useless, a patrol car came around the corner and picked him up. An officer needs assistance call means everyone drops whatever they are doing and goes balls to the wall in an attempt to get there and help. You never know when it might be you that needs help.

The driver of the patrol car shouted, "Hang on junior!"

The two veteran cops in the front seat had obviously done it before. The driver kept the gas pedal to the floor and the passenger called out *clear* at the intersections where there were traffic lights. Partners rely on each other like that. The driver relied on his partner to check the intersections, while he kept his focus up the road. It was the first time Norm had ever driven on city streets like that, blowing red lights at 80 miles an hour.

The car he was in came screeching and sliding to a halt behind several other cop cars that had previously arrived on the scene. The two cops in the front seat bailed out and started to run, but the passenger had to go back and let out Norm who was locked in the back seat. The back doors of cop cars can only be opened from the outside, that keeps the bad guys in.

Norm followed the senior guys into the crowd of hundreds. Some of the crowd started to disperse as the police presence grew. The focus was to get to the cop who needed help, so they had to just push and shove their way through the crowd. Finally, he saw a group of cops in the middle of the melee hovering around a cop who was laying on the ground.

Norm was distracted by the shoves and shouts of the mob, but he noticed that the cop's face and shirt were covered in blood.

The group of cops in the middle of the mob formed a tight circle around their fallen comrade. Then they slowly expanded the circle, pushing the mob back and telling them to disperse at the same time. They were hostile and didn't budge, they just yelled and shook their fists. Some of the cops picked up their injured brother, and then they carried him up and over their heads to get him out of the crowd.

A few of the animals in the mob reached up and grabbed at the injured cop, trying to pull him down. The biggest cop led the way using his riot stick to push through them. For Norm, it was like following a snow plow. The injured cop's face and head were so swollen and bloodied that he didn't recognize him.

Paramedics were waiting near the police cruisers and they took the injured cop to the hospital. Norm and the others returned to the mob telling them to disperse and go home. Some men grabbed the loud-mouthed antagonists and pulled them away. They knew they'd get their heads busted or asses arrested if they didn't. Norm had noticed the whole crowd was of a Middle Eastern descent.

Apparently the off-duty cop was trying to break up a fight amongst them and they thought he was picking on the minorities. Others joined in the fight, and it escalated from there. It was a chain reaction where the mob mentality took over. Norm found out later the injured cop was a fellow rookie who had been hired on just after him. He actually flat lined on the table at the hospital, the severe swelling to his head and brain caused his heart to stop. A jump-start from the doctor brought him back to life.

On the way back to the station in the patrol car, one of the veteran cops up front turned to Norm and said, "Did you learn anything junior?"

"You never let them get you down, they'll put the boots to you."

He felt a little light headed and saw his hands were shaking. He didn't know it at the time, but it was the after-effects of the adrenaline that had been pumping through his veins. When it subsides, you can be left with wobbly knees. Wow, he thought to himself, "I'm sure glad that wasn't me."

Saturday Night's Alright for Fighting

Most normal people run from a fight, but the police have a responsibility to run to it and break it up. Every police officer is taught defensive tactics during their initial training at the police college. Norm's instructor was a martial arts expert who taught the recruits a whole bunch of fancy moves to take down bad guys and how to protect themselves. A lot of the techniques seemed pretty cool, but he had to wonder how effective they would be on the street.

The problem is the same with any sport, if you don't practice and use it, you lose it. Norm tried to practice on his younger siblings at home, but they went crying to mom. He tried using some of the handcuffing techniques while making arrests, but he found they were useless unless the bad guy cooperated. There were a few young women whom Norm had met that wanted to be handcuffed for other reasons.

You may wonder why it sometimes takes four or more cops to successfully take down and hog tie a suspect. It means he is not cooperating or submitting, allowing them to put the cuffs on. Superior manpower helps to ensure the suspect isn't hurt because that is not acceptable in this day and age, no matter what heinous a crime they might have committed.

Norm had been involved in a couple fistfights as a teenager, the kind where the guy that was pinned on the ground would say uncle. He had to stick up for his younger brother in a few neighborhood battles. He was a big kid, his size helped him get the police job. In reality, Norm learned to fight as a cop on the street and while working off-duty in the bars. Even though he was a big man, there was always some other guy who thought he'd go for the title. Liquid courage usually had something to do with it.

The first time he had to hold his own in a fight was after receiving a call for a large party at a housing project. Norm was working by himself and responded to the call during shift change. That meant that he was the only cop in service on the whole east side of the city. He attended to the call and saw about fifty to sixty teenagers drinking and partying right on the street.

A couple of the neighbors approached Norm on his arrival and complained about the loud music, under-age drinking, and public urination. He advised the dispatcher of the situation and asked for back-up while the neighbors continued nattering in his ear. Two guys started to fight on the lawn in front of the townhouses.

One of the neighbors asked Norm, "Aren't you going to do something about that?"

Norm relayed the new information to the dispatcher, knowing full well the nearest help would be at least ten to fifteen minutes away. A few more kids got into the fight and the neighbors demanded that Norm do something about it before someone got hurt. He went around to the trunk of the car, pulled out a three-foot hickory riot stick and swung it up in front of him taking a defensive stance. That shut the neighbors up. He told the dispatcher he was going in and to keep the back up coming.

Norm waded into the crowd that had gathered around the five or six guys that were fighting. He yelled at them to disperse immediately, but his demands were completely ignored. It was a sweltering summer night, and there was a light drizzling rain at the time.

The rain didn't deter the crowd, they were drinking and yelling over the music at the combatants in the fight. Norm approached two teenaged men who were swinging wildly at each other. They were all wet and covered in mud; one of them had no shirt on. Norm got in between the two young men and pushed them apart. One of them disappeared into the crowd, but the shirtless kid took a swing at Norm.

He avoided the punch, then grabbed the kid's extended arm and spun him around, putting him in a headlock. Another kid charged at Norm and slammed into him and the kid knocking him off balance, causing him to lose his grip on his prisoner. Trying to hang on to the wet and muddy kid was like wresting with a greased pig.

The kid reached back in an attempt to pry himself loose, and he knocked Norm's eyeglasses from his face. He was in the middle of the front lawn and he tried to walk the kid back to the police cruiser that was parked at the curb. He had managed to get one handcuff on the kid when he was kicked on his right leg by another kid. Norm reached for his radio microphone but someone knocked it from his hand, it dangled from his belt as he inched his way back to the cruiser.

The same kid that kicked Norm came back at him with his fists raised. He held his prisoner in a headlock with his left arm and swung the riot stick with his right. The blow struck the kid across is raised forearms. He still charged ahead at Norm. He used his prisoner as a shield and whacked the kid with his riot stick again. The blow landed hard on his shoulder and the stick broke in half. Another kid jumped Norm from behind, knocking him to his knees.

Somehow, he managed to hang on to the one handcuffed arm of his prisoner. The kids kept coming, and Norm kept swinging his broken riot stick to keep them back. He heard police sirens coming from a distance, it was a welcome sound.

It seemed like Norm's car was parked a mile away. It was in sight, but it wasn't getting any closer. He swung the riot stick again and broke it again, on the same kid. The kid was relentless and wouldn't back off. The sirens got closer, but the hostile mob was oblivious. Two veteran cops were the first backup to arrive, they grabbed hold of two of the kids who were kicking and punching Norm. They used their prisoners as shields too, keeping their backs to each other while fighting off the rest of the mob.

More cops arrived and one of them chased the kid who was attacking Norm into one of the houses. The crowd started to disperse as the thin blue line got thicker. He finished handcuffing his prisoner and put him in the cruiser. Four more kids were arrested by the other cops. Norm retrieved his mangled glasses from the muddy front lawn and headed for the cop shop.

He had no memory of the ride back to the station. When he got there, one of the other cops laughed out loud and commented when he walked into the report writing room.

"Here comes Buford Pusser."

"You looked just like him in Walking Tall, swinging that big stick."

Another cop added, "Yeah, all we saw when we pulled up was a blue shirt in the middle of the mob swinging a broken riot stick."

Norm laughed and sighed in relief at the same time.

His boss asked, "Hey Norm how's your back?"

He was puzzled and said, "Fine, why?"

"Go look in the mirror."

Norm went into the locker room and looked at himself in the mirror. He had two big muddy shoe prints on the back of his shirt. His shirt was also torn in the front, with mud and someone else's blood spattered on it. His knees and his elbows were all covered in mud and his only injury was a scrape on his left elbow. Norm smiled at himself in the mirror and took solace in the fact he had made it out alive.

The case went to court several months later. Norm was questioned on the witness stand by the lawyer of the one kid's who Norm had whacked with his stick.

The lawyer asked Norm, "Officer, is it true you hit my client with a large wooden baton?"

"Yes sir, a wooden riot stick."

The lawyer stepped closer to the witness stand and raised his voice a bit.

"And how many times did you hit my client with your riot stick officer?"

"At least three times sir, every time he charged at me."

The lawyer stepped up right in front of Norm on the witness stand and raised his voice yet again, for effect.

"And just how hard did you hit my client with your riot stick officer?"

Norm leaned forward in the witness stand, looked over at the judge and said, "As hard as I could."

The other cops and some of the audience in the courtroom chuckled and guffawed. The judge looked directly back at Norm from his lofty perch and just nodded his head.

The kid was found guilty of causing a disturbance by fighting, and resisting arrest. The verdict was the same for the other stupid kids.

Bar Brawls

Norm worked *off-duty* on some weekends in one of the biggest bars in the city. On any given Friday or Saturday night, there were seven to eight hundred rock n' rollers packed into the place. Even though it was a two-cop job, they were still vastly outnumbered. When the cops were first introduced at the bar, Norm had to earn some respect and let the regulars know there was a new sheriff in town. After sizing him up, one of regulars, a local biker, thought *he* would decide when it was closing time.

There was always one loud mouth in the crowd, the rest of the table waited to see how Norm handled their self-designated leader. Norm called a waitress over to the table and started taking away their unfinished drinks, putting them on her tray. The loudmouthed biker got up and retrieved his drink from the tray, but Norm was waiting at his chair and he pulled it away from the table when he went to sit back down. The biker crashed down to the floor and the whole room went silent.

Norm knew better than to let the biker make the first move, so he grabbed him before he could scramble to his feet and put him in a headlock from behind. He kept the biker off balance by dragging him backwards to the side exit, then he pushed him face first through the fire exit door.

Immediately outside the door there was a small porch with a railing. The biker's momentum took him straight into the railing and then over it, head first. He landed upside down in the parking lot. Thinking the problem had been solved, Norm was astounded when he got back to the table and saw the biker charging back in through the front doors. All it took was a nasty Clint Eastwood glare from Norm and the rest of the biker's friends grabbed him and dragged him out of the bar.

They got the message and the new sheriff earned a lot of respect that night.

After closing, one of the owners said to Norm, "I'm glad you're on my side, I wouldn't want those big arms on me."

Norm was working at the megabar one night when his partner showed up late and half in the bag. Poncho was not one of Norm's regular partners at the bar, he was filling in for another guy. He was actually a veteran of the fabled big brawl at another city rock n' roll bar where bodies got tossed through windows out on to the street. Norm considered sending Poncho home but cut him some slack and told him to drink some coffee. The bar was packed as usual.

The owners packed as many people as they could into the place hoping they'd sell more booze. Dealing with the boozing mob was left up to a few bouncers and the two cops. Norm spent most of the night perched near the front door, coincidentally right beside the entrance to the women's restroom. When he wasn't watching the hottie parade, he kept an eye on Poncho and the alcohol absorbing crowd.

Even in a jam-packed bar with blaring rock n' roll music, Norm knew the sound of a fight; it was usually preceded by the sound of breaking glasses falling from the tables. That meant the table had been knocked over and someone was about to duke it out. Scanning the room, he saw the tell-tale crowd gathering around the combatants, not to far from him in the main ballroom. Norm pushed his way through the crowd and grabbed one of the combatants in his signature head lock.

As he tried to back the guy out of the crowd, another guy crashed into them, knocking Norm and the other guy to the floor under some toppled tables. Remembering those words of wisdom that he had once heard, he thought to himself, "I can't let them get me while I'm down."

He hung on to his combatant, using a table as a shield to fend off the kicks from those who were trying to free their buddy and take cheap shots at Norm while he was down.

Poncho had heard the commotion and came to Norm's aid throwing people out of the way. He grabbed a hold of the guy who was after Norm. He will never forget what he saw when he got to his feet. They were surrounded by at least fifty people who were all fighting. Some were trying to help the cops, and others were fighting them. The crowd looked like a churning dark sea, with fists and elbows popping up like white caps.

Norm and Poncho dragged their prisoners up front to the coat room using it as a temporary holding cell. He told the kids who worked in there to keep an eye on the prisoners until they got things under control. He heard sirens in the background and knew that help was on the way. As the number of blue shirts multiplied, the crowd got the message that the fun was over. The band never stopped playing the whole time, it was just another Saturday night fight at the rock n' roll bar.

Norm and his best friend Jesse James earned a good reputation at the bar. That became evident to Norm when he saw the regulars watching their backs when they tossed out troublemakers. The front lobby of the bar was laid out in such a way that it was perfect for bouncing idiots out the door. The walls were covered in thick stucco that had sharp edges. It was great for getting someone's attention when they were shoved up against it.

There were two steps going down to the front doors that helped the evictees gain momentum on their way to the doors. The doors opened out and that was a good thing. The fact they were glass was a bad thing. One night, Norm helped a drunken asshole out the doors, and the poor bastard smashed through one of the glass doors. Miraculously, he did not receive a single cut from the broken glass. But then he decided to come back into the bar through the broken glass door. It was a bloody mess.

The owner later asked, "Oh my God Norm, what can we do so that won't happen again?"

He answered, "Plexiglas would work."

During most nights at the bar, Norm and Jesse *almost* felt guilty collecting a pay cheque for hanging out, chatting about how to get rich outside of police work and admiring the scenery. Then there were those nights that they had to wonder if it was worth the money. Like the night a group of five meatheads thought that they owned the bar. They looked like the offensive line of the Chicago Bears. Two of the five guys were larger than the table they were sitting at, the largest one being well over 300 pounds.

Jesse said to Norm, "I know which one you're getting."

Three of the five were brothers; it was evident by their ugly facial features and girth. They argued with Norm and Jesse while being escorted to the front doors but they eventually took great offence to being kicked out. The fight was on.

Jesse started dancing with the medium sized triplet while the biggest one and another guy grabbed Norm. Jesse had a free hand so he swung his slapper and clipped the one guy in the forehead. Norm struggled with the biggest brother. He found it was impossible to use his famous headlock, the man's head was attached to his shoulders, he had no neck.

Jesse held his own with the brother, but Norm had a hell of a time. His punches just bounced off the guy like he was wailing on a Popeye punching bag. He was built like a brick shithouse without a door. Norm was thankful that the other guys stayed out of it. He was encouraged by that joyful sound of police sirens in the distance.

The big brother was so huge that the cops had to use two pairs of handcuffs linked together to restrain him. The two brothers got to spend the night in jail. It was closing time, so Norm had one of the waitresses patch up his bloodied elbow while he and Jesse enjoyed a couple cold beers. They celebrated another night of staying alive.

Shots Fired

Cops working the street never know what's waiting around the next corner for them. Norm was partnered with a veteran for the midnight shift. They were just loading up their cruiser in the police parking lot at the start of their shift when they heard, "pop, pop…pop." There was no mistaking the sound, it was gunfire. Norm told the dispatcher they were going to check the area for *shots fired*. The shots sounded close by. Norm's partner drove up the block, turned right, and slowed down in front of a neighborhood tavern.

Norm looked to his right, down a dark alley and said, "Down there."

His partner drove down the alley, the cruiser's headlights lit up two men who were fighting up by the side of the building. One man had the other pinned up against the wall, he was punching and kicking him. As Norm's partner pulled closer to the curb, Norm saw something shiny tucked in the back of the one man's waistband.

"Gun!" Norm shouted.

The man's movements seemed to be in slow motion when he reached back for the gun. Norm was already out of the passenger door, charging towards the two men. He grabbed the gun a split second before the guy could and then flattened both men against the wall. He tucked the revolver in the back of his pants and cuffed the guy before he had a chance to turn around.

Norm's partner had the other guy by that time and both men were arrested. Upon closer examination of the gun, Norm saw that it was a snub-nosed .38 caliber, five-shot revolver. There was one empty chamber, and one bullet that had not been fired.

Interviews of the witnesses and the two men laid out an unbelievable sequence of events. The two men had started fighting inside the tavern, then one of them went to his room upstairs and retrieved his gun. The fight continued outside where the man with the gun fired two shots at the other man, but he missed both times. Even more amazing was the fact that the other man took the gun away from him and he fired back, also missing his target. Learning that neither of them could shoot very well, they got back to fist fighting. That's when the cops pulled up.

I See Dead People

Norm saw his share of blood and broken bones while growing up, most of it his own. He will always remember his father bringing him next door to see what a dead man looked like. His elderly neighbor had passed away with Norm's dad at his side. At the suggestion of his father, he reached out and touched the man. He was intrigued by his cold skin and perfect stillness. Cops get to see more than their share of dead people, and Norm was no exception. In most cases, the police are called to investigate a death and to rule out foul play.

It didn't bother Norm, although it was difficult at times trying to pacify the deceased's loved ones who were complete strangers. He was also intrigued by the different circumstances in which some people died. He found people on the toilet, in the bathtub, and in one case, in bed with their spouse who had actually slept the whole night with her dead husband. He was an alcoholic, but she felt bad after calling him a lazy drunken bastard when he refused to get out of bed.

Everyone knows how smelly someone can be when they are alive and cut the cheese. Anyone who has ever smelled a rotting corpse will never forget the distinctively pungent odor that is ten times worse than any good fart. Norm's worst dead body was one found by the landlord of a high-rise apartment building.

The neighbors had complained of a foul smell and he was sent in to investigate. At first glance, Norm thought the body belonged to a three-hundred-pound black man, the skin was chocolate brown and there was what looked like male genitalia visible. It appeared that the man had died after getting out of the shower; a bath robe lay open and underneath the body.

Closer examination revealed the body was actually that of a female, her breasts were stretched beyond recognition and her inner female parts were hanging out. The real shocker to Norm came when the landlord said the body belonged to a white woman in her mid forties.

Ted Masterson explained to Norm how a dead body decomposes: first it bloats, and then it bursts. He was kind enough to warn him of that before he attempted to move the body, he said it would undoubtedly burst. Norm was a little grossed out by the whole ordeal. It was even more disgusting later when he ate lunch and could still smell the odor that had permeated his clothes.

Ted Masterson was a piece of work. Norm recalled seeing the body removal man in action for the first time when he clawed his way through the airplane wreckage at a crash site. It was the most gruesome job he could ever imagine, but the man was a seasoned professional. He still laughs out loud when recalling a war story that he heard from one of the veterans.

The police had been called to an apparent suicide, and accordingly Ted was called for the body removal. One of the cops asked Ted to have a closer look at the victim, since there appeared to be a piece of paper in the guy's mouth. Ted diligently opened the guy's mouth, then he retrieved and unfolded the note. Ted read the note out loud.

It said, "When you're dead, call Ted."

Night of the Living Dead

Seeing dead people really didn't bother Norm. Maybe it was because they weren't bleeding all over him and screaming in agony. Seeing someone in that situation was different and a bit unnerving. One midnight shift, he and his partner were cruising through a residential neighborhood on a dimly lit street. It was a warm and quiet summer night, but then all of a sudden there was a naked woman standing in the middle of the road, like a deer caught in their headlights.

She was a beautiful blonde wearing what looked like a crimson scarf. A click of the high beams revealed that her throat was cut from ear to ear, and blood was gushing down the front of her bare breasts. It looked like a scene from a horror movie, but unfortunately it was real, and she needed help.

Without hesitation, Norm shifted into cop mode. Medical help was summoned and an investigation was launched. At the hospital, he saw the shapely young woman unconscious and laying tits up on a gurney. The doctor said she that had bled out and another minute or two unattended would have cost her life.

He pointed out to Norm what he called a *hesitation mark* alongside the cut on her neck. This was proof the victim inflicted the injury upon herself. According to the doctor, the amount of narcotic she had in her system kept her up and moving, instead of collapsing. As luck would have it, she ran into the cops.

Who said they are never around when you need them?

Twas the Night before Christmas

There was another night that Norm will never forget, it was on a Christmas Eve. Cops are usually busy during the holidays when people are stressed and depressed. He received a domestic disturbance call that was elevated to a stabbing en route. It was a quaint little house in a quiet neighborhood. The house was moderately adorned with colored Christmas lights around the front porch. He and his partner were the second two cops to arrive, at the same time as the ambulance. The other cops were coming out of the front door with a guy in handcuffs as they went in.

The ambulance attendants followed them into the house and immediately attended to a man clad only in sweatpants, lying on the living room floor. The man had several puncture wounds to his abdomen and he was covered in blood. Norm's attention was drawn to the distraught blonde woman who started to spew out an explanation for what had taken place. As she started to talk, Norm noticed her matted hair with streaks of blood in it.

There was spattered blood on over her pink house coat and her hands were covered in the sticky substance that gave off a sulfuric odor. She explained to Norm how her boyfriend had been helping her to wrap her kids' presents when her ex-boyfriend came crashing through the front door, drunk and looking for a fight.

The two men got into it. Words turned into shoving and that turned into punches. Then the ex-boyfriend pulled a knife and plunged it into her boyfriend's abdomen several times. As the woman described the fight, Norm's eyes drifted around the room.

The Christmas tree had been knocked off its stand and it was crushed up against the wall. Some of the presents were trampled, but even worse, they were all spattered with blood. He asked about the kids. The woman said they had been spared from seeing the fight, they were secure in another part of the house. She broke down and started crying.

She said, "What am I going to tell the kids? Look at this place."

One of the other cops, Richard Cranium, overheard her comment and said to his partner,

"We've got to do something about this."

Later, it was well into the night and all the cops involved in the stabbing were busy doing the paperwork back at the station.

Norm asked out loud, "Where the hell is the Dickhead?" *(Richard Cranium's nickname)*

Someone answered and said, "He's on a mission."

Norm assumed he was on a coffee run and thought nothing more of it until the end of the shift when the Dickhead returned. He came into the report room with his arms full of toys he had scrounged from the local hospitals and one store owner who he had apparently dragged out of bed. Yes, the sarcastic bastard that the other cops loved to pick on actually went out and rounded up some new presents for the kids so they'd have something under their tree.

The Dickhead looked at all the other cops in the room and said, "There's no way those kids are gonna miss out on their Christmas."

3
Working the Street

"He Who Knows Others Is Wise. He Who Knows Himself Is Enlightened."

- Tao Te Ching

The best thing about being a rookie is that in time, you won't be one anymore. Somewhere along the line rookie cops lose their virginity, and the experience they gain turns them into seasoned veterans. This was the case with Norm. From walking a beat, he moved into patrol cars as a relief man, filling in for the regular district guys on their days off. That meant he got to work with a different veteran almost every day.

That could be a good or a bad thing depending on who he had to work with. Even with a few years under his belt, Norm was still the rookie in the patrol car. The veterans called the shots on everything, including who would drive and what was for lunch.

The midnight shift was the worst shift to get stuck with a bad partner. One old navy vet who was a raging alcoholic hid booze in the glove box or in his locker. Norm only had to work with him a couple of times. He was almost killed by the drunk early one morning, while on the way into the station after the midnight shift. The ex-sailor had been out all night and was driving in to work pissed drunk.

Norm was on the one-way street leading to the station when a car came at him head on, going the wrong way. He swerved to avoid a collision and saw that it was the drunken sailor behind the wheel of the other car. He felt obligated to do something, so he reported the matter to his sergeant. The sergeant sent the drunken ex-sailor home.

There was another old war vet that Norm had to work with far too often. He always smelled of booze and smoked like a chimney, but nobody ever saw him actually drinking on the job. Perhaps he just came in to work that way. Smoking was quite acceptable at the time, so non-smokers like Norm got to inhale the crap for eight hours straight while in the car.

On one night in particular the guy threw him the keys saying, "You can drive junior."

Norm was excited since the vets usually chose to drive, leaving the rookies to write all the reports. There were no service calls waiting, so he headed out towards their district only to have the guy direct him into a dark parking lot. He couldn't believe it; he was ready to rock, but his partner just wanted to park and sleep all night.

Norm only put up with that once. The next time he waited for the guy to doze off, then he drove around their district purposely hitting every curb and pothole he could find. The guy used his hat as a pillow, but one curb bounced his head off the window and woke him up. Norm tried not to smile, the old guy just scowled and went back to sleep.

There were those quiet nights, when the guys would get bored and play games to amuse themselves. On one such night, Norm's sergeant picked him up from his walking beat. They drove around for a while, then the sergeant pulled up behind another patrol car, purposely rear-ending it.

He grabbed the microphone, and announced over the radio, "You're it."

The sergeant then turned the corner, and raced down an alley. It was called bumper tag…something you could do before they invented air bags. It was also fun *poofing* snow drifts on the side of the road, plowing through them with the car, and watching the fresh snow fly all over. One of the guys was doing it in a store parking lot one night; it was all fun and games, until he hit a shopping cart that was concealed in the snow bank.

Door riding was the most fun, in fresh snow. It was something like the bumper riding you did when you were a kid. In this case the passenger opened the car door, then hopped out using the door for support. The leather soles on the police boots glided perfectly across the packed snow, just like skis.

Rookies walking the beat were always fair game for the veteran car crews. They would pull up to curb and wave the rookie over. Just when the rookie bent over to talk to them, they would blast him with a giant syringe fully loaded with water. They would also sneak up from behind, and toss firecrackers out the car window. It passed the time. On the rare occasion, a car crew would take orders, then drive over the border and pick up a pile of Coney dogs.

Tommy Gunn

Norm got to work with other cops who liked to dig and look for shit to get into. That was just fine by him. Stopping suspicious people and cars made the time pass by quicker. Midnight shifts were brutal when it was quiet. Norm got to work with Tommy Gunn quite a bit. He was a go getter whose nickname was for his big mouth, and the fact that he loved to bullshit.

When Tommy told a war story, the guys who were actually there just laughed, because it was nowhere near the truth. Regardless, Tommy liked to work. Norm learned how to, and how not to, working with Tommy. Working as partners, He and Tommy received two separate commendations for their diligent police work during a break-in at a business and after a robbery at a gas bar.

One night while Tommy and Norm were on routine patrol, the dispatcher sent them to assist the fire department at a house fire. Usually that meant the police were needed for crowd control or traffic direction. They were only a couple blocks from the call. Norm just about shit when they drove around the corner and he saw that the house was on fire and there were no fire personnel on the scene.

He saw thick grey smoke coming out of the upstairs windows and the open front door of the two-story frame house. A woman stood on the front lawn waving frantically and screaming that her children were in the house. Tommy and Norm ran to the front door and then into the front hallway. The woman had told them her children were upstairs in the house.

A wall of thick black smoke knocked both cops to the floor. They tried to crawl up the stairs in the hallway, but the smoke and heat from the fire drove them back outside. While Norm gasped for air, Tommy screamed on the radio for the dispatcher to send the fire department, police back-up, ambulances, the media, and the National Guard. Well, maybe he didn't ask for the army, but Tommy did get overly excited.

As Tommy called for help, two young boys appeared in the upstairs window, up above the front porch and door. Tommy waved and yelled for the boys to jump out the window to them on the porch. Just then a long haired, skinny white guy pushed his way past Norm and ran into the house. He pursued and tackled the guy in the hallway inside the house.

The guy resisted and yelled, "Let it burn, let it burn!"

As Norm dragged the guy out the door, one of the boys climbed out the window. He tossed the guy over the porch railing like a sack of potatoes, he landed on the front lawn.

One of the young boys jumped from the window into their arms. They handed the boy to their mother, then Tommy yelled up to his brother to jump down. Norm saw an orange glow in the room behind the boy and thick black smoke billowing out the window over his head. He looked terrified and he was crying. He disappeared from the window. The mother and Tommy both went berserk.

The mother screamed for her son and Tommy screamed for an oxygen mask so he could go into the house. Norm looked into the hallway. It looked like the depths of hell, he saw nothing but fire and smoke. There was no way to get into the house without getting cooked alive. Just then a fire rescue truck pulled up. Tommy almost pulled the mask off one of the firefighters, he told them there was a child upstairs in the house.

Most people run out of a burning house. Norm gained a new respect for firefighters that day as two of them ran into the burning house. They disappeared through into the inferno.

The dirt bag on the front lawn got back to his feet and charged back up the porch. Norm grabbed him again, then cuffed him and stuffed him into the cop car. More fire trucks and cops arrived; the boy upstairs was still not visible. Norm saw that flames had broken through the roof and were now shooting out of the window above the porch.

The heat was so intense that he felt like his forehead was melting. The firefighters appeared to be running around aimlessly while they tried to establish water lines. Nobody reacted to the sound of an oxygen tank alarm going off inside of the house. One of the firefighters who was inside the house waved out a side window from upstairs, he was out of air. Two cops ran to a fire truck and grabbed a ladder, they helped firefighters prop it up against the house to reach the upstairs window.

The firefighter in the window had the second little boy in his arms; he hung him out the window by one arm, he looked like a rag doll just dangling there. The boy had only his pajama bottoms on and he was blackened with soot from the waist up. He was handed down the ladder to the other firefighters and cops below. The firefighter on the ladder then reached up to help his comrade out of the window. He had his mask off and he hung his head out the window gasping for air.

Thick black smoke billowed out the window over his head. Blue and orange flames chased him out the window and on to the ladder. Backing down the ladder, the firefighters slipped and came crashing down on top of the other men below.

Norm heard the aluminum siding on the house crackling from the intense heat. Then he heard the sound of glass breaking, and someone shouted, "Look out!"

A giant black and orange fireball exploded through the front picture window, over the porch and across the front lawn. The scene unfolded in slow motion as Norm watched the fire and glass flying through the air, and everyone diving for cover. The fireball mushroomed out into the night air, barely over the heads of firefighters and police who were sprawled out on the front lawn.

The roaring sound almost popped his ears. It was ten times louder than that *whoomph* sound you hear after pouring gasoline onto a bonfire. Everyone had to back off because of the intensity of the heat. The house was lost, it went up like a cardboard schoolhouse, one of those fireworks you lit up as a kid. It burned to the ground.

Both boys suffered from smoke inhalation, and a couple of firefighters got banged up, but there were no serious injuries. As it turned out, the dirt bag Norm arrested was who set the fire. He was the downstairs tenant, whom the mother had left in charge of her two boys while she went out. He had intentionally set the fire and was subsequently charged with Arson.

Months later in court, the prosecuting attorney pulled Tommy and Norm aside asking if they had been at the same fire. Apparently, Tommy was on a roll trying to impress the jury with his heroics, telling them how he dashed through the flaming inferno and saved the day. In reality, it was a scary experience for everyone involved. It was a great combined effort by the police and firemen. For years, the two organizations had an ongoing rivalry, so it was great to see how well everyone worked together.

Tommy's naked curiosity caught up to him several years later when he got himself arrested for allegedly sexually assaulting female prostitutes. Norm had never thought much about Tommy's behavior when he'd search city parks or the *passion pits* looking for couples getting it on in their cars.

He would say that they had to check for under age women or possible rape victims. Tommy made them get out of their cars before they had a chance to put their clothes back on. Norm thought that part was a little strange, especially on one occasion with two gay guys.

Motor Town

Norm worked downtown and on the west side for his first seven years in uniform, then he was transferred to the east side station. The east side was mostly quieter, with the exception of the Ford Road area in Motor Town. The area was actually a city itself, prior to annexation decades earlier.

It was a gritty neighborhood surrounded by three automotive manufacturers and some of their parts suppliers. Ford road ran down the middle. At one time, it was lined with a dozen bars and bootleggers in less than a quarter mile. Some private citizens had make shift bars in their homes where the factory workers could quaff a couple of beers on their lunch hour, day or night. Illegal booze had flowed through the city since the days of Al Capone, he frequented the city back in the rum running days of prohibition.

Working out of a new station meant a new totem pole for Norm to climb. Being the junior man on the platoon also meant he was last to pick vacation time. Norm was told he could pick any of the weeks in November or February that he wanted, that was it. The bottom job on the night shift was working in the office doing mostly secretarial work. The only time he got out of the office was when someone called for the paddy wagon.

On one particular night Norm and the paddy wagon were called to a large house party that had gotten out of hand. All the east side patrol cars were on the scene trying to coral hundreds of party goers who had spilled out on to the street.

On arrival he saw some of the neighbors sitting out front of their houses on lawn chairs watching the action. Several of the neighbors had complained of the loud music, noise, and fighting, along with kids urinating and vomiting on their property. The first responding patrol car had asked the house owner to turn the music down and disperse some of his guests, but the request was ignored.

The east side sergeant was also on the scene and he called for a team huddle. He told Norm to back the paddy wagon up to the front of the house.

He said to the guys, "Shut it down."

Norm backed the wagon up as ordered and opened up the back doors for business. Some of the crowd saw that as their cue to leave the party, but a hard-core group of assholes near the front porch started hurling beer bottles and obscenities at the cops on the street. The boys in blue moved in and started to clean house.

The blue broom crew swept up the porch and into the house, pushing and shoving stubborn partiers aside. Pushes and shoves escalated into punches and kicks. Norm began to receive his first paddy wagon guests as the party idiots and morons were arrested and handcuffed.

He heard an awful commotion coming from inside the house, the fight was on.

One of the cops came out the front door and yelled, "Hey Norm, catch!"

Some poor bastard got tossed across the porch and over the first three steps without touching down. He bounced off the bottom step and landed in a crumpled heap at Norm's feet. Without hesitation, he snatched him up and tossed him head first into the paddy wagon. One by one, more bodies came flying out the door, air mailed to Norm. He thought the action was pretty cool until the paddy wagon was full and the idiots inside started fighting with each other.

The downtown paddy wagon had to be called while Norm took his full load to the east side station. The brawl in the back of the paddy wagon got so bad they almost tipped the van over in one turn, two wheels came right off the ground as Norm rounded a corner. He was freaked out, but nervously laughed it off.

The officer in charge of the station greeted Norm in the garage, asking him how many prisoners he had. Norm admitted he really didn't know. Fifteen drunken, beat up, dirt bags were removed one by one from the wagon. The problem was there were only seven, single jail cells in the whole police station. The young men had to be stacked two and three to a cell while some of them were still fighting.

Once the whole gang was locked up, Norm had to register them all in the cellblock ledger. The first guy stepped up to the counter, he was bleeding from his nose and had a swollen lip and right eye.

The strait-laced officer in charge said, "What happened to you, young man?"

The guy replied, "I fell down the stairs."

The second guy stepped up with soiled and torn clothes, a big clump of his hair missing and a big scuff mark on his left cheek.

The boss asked again what happened, and the second guy said, "I fell down the stairs."

The third guy stepped to the counter; he looked like he had just been run over by a truck.

The boss asked him to sign some paperwork but the third guy said, "I can't, my fingers are all broken."

The boss asked, "I suppose you fell down the stairs too?"

The third guy answered, "Yeah, how do you know that?"

Norm just about pissed himself right there. The boss walked away shaking his head in disgust. Norm didn't laugh the rest of the night while he processed the pile of paperwork. He had each of the different arresting officers' parade through the cell block claiming who had arrested who. There were a couple of the poor bastards left unclaimed. Norm just assigned them to someone.

Ford Road

Police work wasn't all about fighting. When Norm wasn't doing paperwork, he put in hours and hours on patrol. Sometimes he would drive for eight hours, not receiving a single call for service. Lunch hours were an hour long so he was able to work out in the gym at the station and keep himself buffed up.

As the years passed, the city got busier and Norm was sent from call, to call, to call. Back when he was hired, there was no driver training, so cops learned how to drive on the job. Sure, anyone with a license can drive a car, but only race car drivers and veteran cops know how their cars really perform and how they can drive them aggressively at excessive speeds. Race car drivers are confined to a racetrack, but cops have to get places as quickly and as safely as possible while dodging a myriad of obstacles and some other, very stupid drivers.

On one sunny summer day, Norm was dispatched to a motor vehicle accident with injuries. That meant lights and sirens en route. He sped down a multi-lane road where everyone ahead of him was pulling over into the right lane, like they were supposed to do.

Well, not everyone has common sense. A woman driver who was already in the right lane decided she'd pull out into the left lane, directly into Norm's path. There was a solid row of cars to the right and a huge cement pole on the left. He chose the path of least resistance and plowed into the rear end of the stunned woman's car. That was to be his only motor vehicle accident in his entire career, and it wasn't his fault.

Norm liked the action that came with working the Motor Town district. It wasn't a steady assignment for him until Buck Flynn's partner booked off with a long-term illness. Norm asked, and Buck agreed to take him on as a temporary partner. Buck was a hard-nosed cop from the old school. His Dirty Harry stare alone could frighten the bad guys, but he had a heart of gold when it came to helping others. Buck was occasionally moody so Norm would get in his face and say, "So what's the bug up your ass today?"

It would be just the elbow to the ribs Buck needed to open up and get the problem off his chest. Buck liked sticking it to dirt bags and that was just fine by Norm. Their strategy was to try and make their lives as miserable as the victims of their crimes. Norm always hated being assigned to jobs like parking or radar enforcement, he just wanted to lock up bad guys.

There was no shortage of prey for them around Ford Road. It was like shooting fish in a barrel at times. There was even a biker clubhouse in the neighborhood to keep an eye on. The city had three biker gangs, one with their clubhouse on Ford Road. They stopped one of the other gang's enforcers one day and welcomed him to the hood with a ticket for not wearing his seat belt (he was driving a car). The biker was no stranger to getting hassled by the cops. Norm was puzzled when he handed him the ticket and the biker said,

"Why don't you just airmail me like everyone else does?"

Norm and Buck had a good chuckle. Some cops wrote tickets for certain dirt bags and did not turn them in. The ticket then became an arrest warrant when it went unpaid, and the dirt bag got arrested for a ticket he had never received. The law worked in mysterious ways.

One night, Norm was called to the biker clubhouse for a murder. A couple of the neighborhood punks had lured the club president out of the clubhouse and into a vacant lot where they caved his head in with baseball bats.

It was a tough neighborhood where the kids weren't even afraid of the bikers. The two killers were arrested and sent to jail with life sentences. In Canada that means you can be out in seven years with good behavior. That was the case with Donny Gates, he was a convicted murderer, yet he was allowed back in the very neighborhood where he killed a man.

Donny had parole conditions, one being not to associate with any other know criminals. What a joke that was, *all* of Donny's friends were known criminals. Norm made it a point to stay on Donny's ass, and he arrested him for breaching the conditions of his parole on three separate occasions.

Each and every time the courts put him back on the street. His lawyer said that Norm was picking on his client. A few years later, Donny Gates savagely beat his girlfriend to death during a drug induced rage. He went back to jail for his second murder. Society finally realized Donny was a bad man and he was designated as a dangerous offender. This meant he'd have to spend the rest of his life in jail, for real.

On the Light Side

Cops are only human. Seeing the things they do and dealing with people at their worst, can take its toll on anyone. Veteran street cops become seasoned, but also callous. People never call the police when they're having a good day. They deal with all the world's ills and yet they are expected to remain polite and courteous at all times.

You always hear about someone who ran into a cop having a bad day. For all you know, his previous call could have been a sexually abused child. Cops have feelings too.

Cops have a sense of humor, and so did Norm. For that matter, he found that it broke the tension in many situations and it helped him deal with the worst in people that he saw on a daily basis. Some people would appreciate Norm's sense of humor in the right situation, others just thought he was being sarcastic. Norm got to work with the king of jokers on one Halloween night.

Cuckoo Connors brought in a Porky Pig mask to wear while out on patrol. A uniformed cop wearing a Pig mask. Norm had to play the straight guy, driving the cruiser, with Cuckoo as his pig-headed partner. The reactions from the public were off the charts. Norm stopped at a red light beside another car and the driver casually glanced over, nobody likes to eyeball the cops directly. The guy and his passenger laughed so hard they forgot to go when the light changed to green.

While driving past other cars, some drivers rubber-necked so hard they swerved into oncoming traffic. Cuckoo and Norm stopped at one of the local bars and did a walk through; Norm kept his dead serious cop look, and Cuckoo just being Porky Pig.

Eyes popped out of heads, jaws dropped, and one guy spewed his drink all over his friends. Oddly enough, there were a few people who obviously had *no* sense of humor, they just stared in disbelief with a look of horror on their faces.

Practical jokes were always a great way to pass the quiet time and to have some fun. Norm loved a good practical joke, especially if it was at someone else's expense. Lucky for him, Richard Cranium was on his shift one year. The Dickhead was everyone's favorite target. Norm and his partner Digger Daniels secretly played pranks on both the Dickhead and his partner.

It was hilarious because one always expected it was the other that was doing the pranks. It started with packing the partner's car full of leafs, collected from bags placed at the side of the road. The cops who were in on the prank all hid in the parking lot watching the poor bastard try to pull all the leaves out of his car so he could go home.

Naturally, a payback had to be planned so Digger rigged the Dickhead's car with a special device. Again, the other cops hid in the parking lot while the Dickhead tried to start his car. A shrieking sound came from the engine, followed by a popping sound and a lot of smoke. He leaped from his car, running in circles with his hands in the air.

He gingerly approached the hood and then stopped to look back; he could hear the howling coming from the other parked cars. Simple and/or elaborate, the pranks carried on. Norm tried to rig the partner's locker with firecrackers but he accidentally set his police uniforms on fire. Retaliation was shoe polish rubbed around the inside brim of the Dickhead's hat. When he removed his hat, he had a lovely black halo around his forehead.

The Dickhead and his partner continually denied pulling pranks on each other and decided it was best to call a truce. Digger and Norm left the station early one day and went straight to the local variety store where the Dickhead stopped for a cigar every day. Digger convinced the store clerk to let him put a special load in the Dickhead's cigar, then the clerk placed it back in the box. It was too bad only the Dickhead's partner got to see it.

He went to the store as usual and purchased his special cigar. His partner had no problem keeping a straight face since he had no idea of what was about to happen. The two cops started gabbing while on patrol and the Dickhead lit up his cigar. He was on his third big puff when *kaboom!* The cigar blew up in the Dickhead's face. His partner burst into laughter and almost lost control of the car. The truce was over.

Gut Instincts

Seasoned street cops develop a sixth sense when it comes to things like cruising in a patrol car or seeing someone run a stop sign four blocks up the road. They use their peripheral vision, noticing things that anyone else would take for granted. It is the same with gut instinct. Norm was told when he started on the job that good common sense would carry him through his career. Good instincts made him a better cop.

Anyone can have a gut instinct about certain things. The key is to learn how to rely on those instincts, since they are usually well-founded. Norm always remembered one of his old war vet sergeants who would pick him up on the walking beat. It was in the middle of the winter and the sergeant had all the windows down.

He said, "It's to hear the sound of breaking glass, my son."

This was the same man who took Norm into a coffee shop and he sucked back a piping hot coffee before Norm even got his coat off.

Buck and Norm were less than an hour into their afternoon shift, just cruising up Ford Road into the bowels of Motor Town. Both cops' eyes locked on to a beater entering the alley from a hotel parking lot. Seasoned dirt bags frequently drive the back roads and alleys to avoid any attention from the police. Buck and Norm always made a point of driving down those back roads and alleys.

Norm drove parallel to the beater for the length of the block where it turned on to a side street off of Ford. There were two guys in the beater and they didn't see the cops until they crossed Ford directly in front of them. They had already made their decision to pull the beater over so Norm switched on the roof lights.

The chase was on.

The driver accelerated and ran a stop sign at the first side street. The car slid sideways making the right turn. The passenger lobbed full beer bottles like hand grenades back at the cop car. Buck radioed in the chase while Norm focused on the fleeing car and the road ahead of him. The driver circled around the neighborhood trying to lose the cops; they were hot on his tail. Speeds got up to sixty miles per hour on the residential side streets.

The driver lost control at one point and drove over the front lawns of three houses. One horrified resident ran for his life. The spinning tires on the dirt and dry grass caused such a dust cloud Norm could barely see the fleeing car. At one point, an apple and banana from Norm's lunch bag rolled up from the back seat and got lodged under the gas pedal.

Buck just gave Norm his Dirty Harry scowl and shouted, "Don't lose this guy!"

The driver of the beater barely let up off the gas pedal as he blew through stop signs and slid sideways around corners. Norm was driving a shitty cruiser that stalled in one turn, he had to drive with both feet to keep it from stalling again.

The adrenalin pumped through Norm's veins, he noticed he was barely sitting on the seat as he handled the steering wheel and pounded down the accelerator. He looked up ahead of the beater and saw that another cruiser had blocked the road.

The two cops were positioned on either side of their cruiser with their guns aimed at the speeding car that was bearing down on them. The fleeing driver continued accelerating, aiming his car at one of the cops. He dove behind his cruiser to avoid getting run down; the beater mounted the curb and drove over the sidewalk, continuing down into a viaduct and intersecting main road.

He went north on Ford and then turned east on River Road. Rush hour traffic clogged the eastbound lane, so the driver passed the back-up in the oncoming lane forcing any westbound vehicles off the road.

The beater then turned back south. Norm was gaining on him so he told Buck he'd try to take him out when he made another turn. Buck was busy hanging out the passenger window shooting at the fleeing car while Norm sped up and tried to P.I.T. the car. He saw one of Buck's bullets hit the trunk dead center just as the beater missed his right turn onto another main artery.

The beater crashed through some wooden construction barricades in the oncoming lane, and it sideswiped an eastbound car that was stopped at the traffic light. Pieces of broken wood rained down on the cruiser. Norm slowed down thinking he couldn't make it between the cars and median.

Buck shouted, "Go, Go!"

Norm sideswiped the same car, but continued the pursuit. The beater only went a few more blocks, then the driver wheeled it into a parking lot. Both he and passenger bailed out on foot and ran. Buck fired a shot that struck the passenger door. That guy stopped dead in his tracks. The driver ran from the car so Norm had to chase him on foot.

He ran down an alley and then into some back yards. He hopped over fences, going from yard to yard. Norm tried to keep up and he got yelled at by an old lady as he ran through her garden. In the next yard, the guy caught the attention of a Pit Bull on his way over the fence. Norm couldn't stop and the dog nipped his ass as he ambled over the fence.

The young dude was too quick for Norm, but he couldn't outrun the police radio. Jesse James and two other cops were waiting for the guy at the end of the block and they put the grab on him when he exited the last yard. Norm was so jacked up on adrenaline he almost tore the back door off Jesse's cruiser after stuffing the guy into the back seat.

Jesse asked, "Are you okay Norm?"

He could only manage a grin and a nod while trying to catch his breath. Jesse shrugged and laughed out loud.

Buck and Norm sat down on a curb in the parking lot near the car with the fresh bullet holes. They wound down, nodding at each other in satisfaction of a job well done.

Norm pointed at the bullet hole in the car's passenger door and commented to Buck, "So that's how you got your guy to stop."

Buck just smiled and gave out one last order.

He waved a neighborhood kid over and said, "Here kid, take two bucks and go buy us a couple of Pepsis'."

During a search of the car, they found more beer and a replica hand gun in the glove box. Why did they run and what were they up to? Those were the questions that had to be addressed when they reported the chase to their boss. The only excuse the driver gave them for running was that he didn't have a license or insurance.

Their instincts led them to believe there was more to his story, but it remained a mystery. About an hour or so later, the cell man came into the report writing room with a big shit eating grin on his face. He said the driver had confessed to him. As it turned out, the driver was on the lam; he was an escaped convict from a prison in British Columbia.

The chase made the local newspaper. They quoted Buck in saying, "The guy driving the car was as dangerous as someone waving a machine gun around."

That quote probably saved Buck and Norm from any criminal or police act charges for the shooting and property damage. High speed chases were being seriously scrutinized by the politicians of the day; they were trying to outlaw them completely.

Later that same year, new government legislation was passed prohibiting the police from shooting from their moving vehicles. Further guidelines were attached limiting the police as to who they could and could not pursue. It was one more advantage the system gave the criminals over the police.

4
Squeaky Sally

After fifteen years in a police uniform Norm was transferred to the Drug Squad. Now he got to work in plain clothes and do investigative work. It took him a few years longer to get into the Drug Squad than the others who were junior to him and already in the unit. He was never an ass kisser and had apparently burned a few bridges along the way.

The man in charge of the entire Investigation Division, Ash Kist, was one for sure. Norm got this first hand from a guy whose job in the Surveillance Unit was up for grabs. He went right to Kist's office, closed the door, and asked him what the problem was. Kist turned beat red and squirmed in his chair. He was adamant there were no ill feelings, but he was more interested in where Norm got his information from. Not an hour after he left Kist's office, his source called back asking what the hell he had said to him. He was now on a witch hunt to find the leak. Norm had repeatedly applied for other plain clothes jobs. Thanks to a different boss, he eventually landed the job in the Drug Squad.

On his first day in the Drug Squad Norm felt a bit lost, but he knew he would eventually flourish there. The squad was filled with type A personalities. He had never considered himself to be in that category, but he later learned that he was. Everyone carried their own files and conducted their own investigations into suspected or known drug dealers and their associates. Norm had gotten to know the specific bad guys in the areas that he had worked, but the new influx of drug information was overwhelming. The veterans in the office always seemed to be on the phone talking to someone named Buddy. He soon learned that this was the common nickname that they used for all their informants, so that their true identities could be kept confidential. That had to be done to ensure the safety of the confidential informants, or C.I.'s.

Norm learned how not to act, or look like a cop, to be able to blend in while doing surveillance. He thought it was great to be able to go to work in jeans and a t-shirt. He also had to learn a whole new language: drug names, terms, slang, and the sub-cultures that went along with drugs like heroin, cocaine, and marihuana.

Like so many other honest professionals, Norm had experimented with some drugs prior to becoming a cop. He was not naïve but admittedly amazed at the amount of drug trafficking in the city. The Drug Squad was the only place he ever worked where everyone scrambled to answer the phone. They just never knew if that big tip was the next incoming call. For the most part, the Drug Squad was a self-motivated unit. Officers received information on drug trafficking from various sources, then they investigated. The main source of good information came from informants, they are the lifeblood of good drug investigators.

As an investigator, you have to consider the informant's motivation, or reason for supplying the police with information. There is always a reason. Motivators can be money, revenge, elimination of the competition, dismissal of or leniency on existing criminal charges or traffic tickets. Sometimes they are just do-gooders. It is important to know exactly why someone wants to become a rat.

Piccadilly Circus

After about three months of learning the ropes, Norm got his call. It was from a woman who identified herself as Sally. She told Norm that she was an opiate abuser who had turned to prostitution to supply her daily dilaudid habit. She was sick of the lifestyle and wanted to get into a methadone maintenance program.

Norm met Sally and she supplied him with twenty-six names of people who were involved in the dilaudid sub-culture, drug dealers and users. She explained to Norm how heroin was almost impossible to get in the city, so everyone turned to dilaudid. You could take the pills orally, but the method of choice was by injection.

Heroin, opium, morphine, dilaudid, oxycontin, and methadone are all opiates, meaning they are derived from the opium poppy, or the seed resin in that plant. Heroin and opium were once prescribed for pain by physicians around and after the turn of the century, but they found that the drugs were addictive. Morphine was widely used during the Second World War for serious battlefield injuries, but they found that it too was addictive.

Synthetic heroin or dilaudid is six to eight times more potent than morphine. It is prescribed to terminal cancer patients. Addicts discovered that dilaudid was easier to get than heroin and much safer to use. Oxycontin is the new dilaudid on the streets today. Methadone is a legally prescribed substitute drug used to wean addicts off the illegal narcotics.

Norm was mesmerized as he listened to Sally ramble on for two hours. Her daily routine consisted of working the street, finding a John to have sex with, and then using the money to buy dilaudid so she could get high. She would repeat this cycle throughout the day, every day. She was physically addicted to dilaudid and would get sick if she didn't get her fix. Sally knew where, and from whom to buy dilaudid on the street. Norm took all the information Sally gave him and created an intelligence file that he called, "Piccadilly Circus." It was a binder full of dilaudid dealers and users with their names, photos, and addresses.

On one occasion, Norm and his file were called to court by the defense counsel in a murder trial. A dillyhead had murdered an old man for his money and pills. The arrogant lead detective *(Richard Cranium)* didn't have a grasp on how desperate a dilaudid addict could be. The defense lawyer was fishing to see if his client was in the Piccadilly Circus file, but privacy issues prevented him from actually looking into the file. Norm thought that it was all quite interesting. The Dickhead wasn't amused.

A Bulge in his Pants

The day after meeting Sally, Norm put her to work. She went about her day hooking and getting high, while gathering information as to who was holding dilaudid. Sally paged Norm around mid-day and said that Paula Watson was selling #4 dillies *(four milligram pills)* for fifty dollars each.

Information had to be recent and confirmed before a search warrant could be obtained to search someone's home. Norm got fifty dollars in buy money from his boss and went out to meet Sally. He drove her to Paula's house and gave her the fifty bucks to make a buy. Within five minutes Sally returned to the van with one #4 dilaudid pill. She said that Paula retrieved the pill from a bottle she was hiding in her bra. Norm had been working the day shift which normally ended at 5:00pm. That was only fifteen minutes away. If he wanted to bust Paula, it meant obtaining a search warrant to search her residence. It was quitting time at any other normal job. In the drug cop world, you don't go home until the dealer is locked up and the paper work is done.

It was time for Norm to write his first search warrant. Granted, warrants were much easier to obtain way back when, but this was B.C. *(before computers)* and everything had to be typed in quadruplicate, using carbon paper, on one of those old machines known as a typewriter. Thank God he had taken one year of typing in high school.

The next obstacle to obtaining a warrant is getting it signed by a judge, they all go home at 4:00pm. That meant Norm had to drive a half an hour out of town to see the judge at their home. He had to wait while the judge read the warrant and decided whether or not it met the criteria for them to sign it.

The warrant was granted and at precisely 6:35pm Norm and the Drug Squad pushed their way through Paula's front door. Stealth is very important in entering someone's house if you want to grab them before they dump or destroy any of the drugs or other evidence. In this case, Paula's father-in-law Brownie answered the door for the female squad member and they pushed their way in past him.

Searching someone's home for drugs is not fun by any means. Just try to imagine someone hiding small pills about the size of children's aspirin somewhere in their house, and then you have to try to find it. It could take hours and experienced drug dealers like Paula don't offer you any help whatsoever.

Norm found one dilaudid pill in the pants of a clown doll that was on a display stand in Paula's bedroom. He later found some more hidden in the hem of her living room curtains.

Several months later during Paula's trial, Norm was on the witness stand testifying in court as to how and where he found the pills. There he stood in the hushed courtroom, holding the clown in his hands, showing the courtroom how he had felt a bulge in the clown's pants. Norm heard more than a few chuckles from the audience in the court room and his colleague Bongo burst out in laughter. He had to leave the courtroom.

Sally had now proven herself as a reliable source and a valuable informant. She was probably cute in her younger days with shiny blonde hair, blue eyes and a few freckles. Hard living aged and ravaged her girlish appearance, but she had a big heart and was soft spoken with a little mouse voice. Looking at her, you would never imagine anyone paying her for sex.

When she called the office for Norm one time, one of the guys said, "Hey Norm, there's some squeaky chick on the phone for you."

Thus, she became known as "Squeaky Sally." She seemed quite simple to Norm. He later learned from her mother that Sally suffered from fetal alcohol syndrome, one of those lovely things you can pass on to your children when you abuse alcohol while you're pregnant. Sally managed to get by with government assistance in the form of a disability check.

Ma Barker

Norm's next target was a crotchety old woman people on the street referred to as Ma. Her last name really wasn't Barker, but it will be used here to protect the identity of the nasty old bitch. Ma was a grandmother and second-generation welfare scammer who abused the system any which way she could. Out of the kindness of her heart, she let street people shack up at her place.

Of course, they were expected to chip in and help pay the bills by either selling drugs, stealing shit, or by prostituting themselves. Norm referred to her place as Ma's half-way whorehouse. Sally occasionally stayed at Ma's when she was down and out. Ma was an enabler for Sally's addiction.

Sally supplied Norm with information on Ma Barker that led to her arrest on three separate occasions. Ma never got off the couch the whole time her home was being searched. On one occasion, it was because the dilaudid was hidden in the hollow leg of the coffee table directly in front of her. She called Norm everything but a white man that day.

Ma's drug charges piled high enough that she eventually had to appear in court to answer for her lawless ways. It was a sight to behold, she was decked out in her best Sunday church dress and carrying an oxygen tank. Norm suggested to her she might want to put out the cigarette she was smoking before she blew up the courthouse.

The swift hammer of justice came down on Ma and she was sentenced to a lengthy term of double secret probation. Par for the course for a softhearted, poor old grandmother on her deathbed.

Mack Attack

Sally continued to feed Norm intelligence information for his "Piccadilly Circus" file. She told him about a well-known, weasel of a dirt bag Norm had arrested back in his uniform days. Mack Crow was one of Sally's steady suppliers of dilaudid. She said he especially like dealing to the hookers because he tried to get his dick licked in the process of making a drug deal.

Mack was a guy who probably always had to pay for sex, he was butt ugly. His face looked like a can of smashed ass. He was short and skinny with lots of tattoos, and his long hair was greasy enough to be a fire hazard. He had a Pee Wee Herman voice and a downright bad attitude toward everyone and everything in the world.

Mack's record card consisted of pages of criminal convictions for stuff like theft, robbery, assault, and drug trafficking. Calling him a shit bag would be considered being polite. Oh yes, and one more thing, Mack just happened to be Ma Barker's son. It seemed Ma was too ill to carry on the family business so Mack took it over.

Sally told Norm that Mack was running a shooting gallery at his house. Another pre-cursor to searching an unknown house is that you have to do some reconnaissance of the building and surrounding area. You can rely somewhat on a description of the building interior from the informant, but someone has to physically reconnoiter the area to find the best approach, and point of entry. Some of the many things that have to be considered are:

Where do you park the vehicles so your presence won't be compromised?

Where do you stage or get the team into formation prior to the entry?

Which door will you use to get into the building?

Who is in the house?

Are there any children?

Are there dogs or firearms?

The list goes on. Then, no matter how perfect the plan is, you have to be prepared for something to go wrong. For drug cops, it seems that something always goes wrong.

Sally supplied Norm with a rough layout of Mack's house. Norm drew it and the operational plan on an eraser board to brief the other officers. Mack was known to have or carry guns, so in this case, the S.W.A.T. team was called in to assist with the initial entry and clearing of the house for possible threats.

It's nice to have the S.W.A.T. team if you think there is a weapon involved. If someone is going to take a bullet on the way in the door, it will be one of them. Some of the guys actually get off on that thought. Because of the weapon threat, the decision was made to use a stealth approach to the house and then a dynamic entry. The S.W.A.T. team loves dynamic entries because they get to don face masks and automatic weapons, then crash through the door scaring the shit out of everyone, while throwing them to the floor at gunpoint. It is a rush for adrenaline junkies.

The approach to the house had to be done very quietly as not to tip off the occupants and have any potential evidence destroyed. It was a very busy neighborhood with lots of pedestrian traffic, some of which was going in and out of Mack's house. Norm's drug team followed the S.W.A.T. team from the dark alley at the rear of the house into the back yard.

The S.W.A.T. guys get all geared up and geeked up in preparation for a raid. It's like a football team getting pumped up before a game. They have about thirty pounds of special equipment on and their adrenaline starts pumping through their veins as they anticipate the start of the game. Adrenaline is a wonderful drug, but rising levels of it in your bloodstream can cause tunnel vision, and in some cases partial hearing loss. This is the reason why many people who have been involved in a shooting say they never heard the gunshot.

So, what happens some time and what happened on that night, was that one of the S.W.A.T. guys was so geeked up he didn't realize how noisy he was being when the teams lined up along the side of the house. He accidentally slammed up against the house instead of just leaning against it. Norm had been listening to the action inside the house through an open window, but all went silent with the bang on the side of the house.

In a dynamic entry, you have six to eight seconds to get in and get control before you lose the element of surprise.

Norm shouted, "Go, Go, Go!"

He waved the S.W.A.T. guys up to the front porch. They crashed through the door and did their thing inside, clearing any potential threats. Norm and his guys then went in and found everyone spread eagle, face down on the living room and kitchen floors.

Bathing Beauty

One of the S.W.A.T. guys stood in the bathroom doorway and he motioned his head for Norm to come over. He pointed his gun into the bath tub that was partially obscured by the shower curtain. He saw that someone was hiding in the tub and he pulled back the curtain. There was Squeaky Sally, naked as the day she was born. She was on her elbows and knees with her cottage cheese ass sticking up in the air and her face down covered by her hands.

Apparently, she was trying to be invisible, like when you were a kid. It was a sight, she had more stretch marks around her mid-section than a thirty-year-old leather sofa. Norm tried not to smirk when he told her to get up and put her clothes on *(he remembered her saying she had to give up her child when she gave birth at sixteen).* Upon exiting the tub, she told Norm that Mack made her strip naked to check for wires or to see if she was bugged. It was his way of getting a cheap thrill.

Sally briefed Norm as to who was who in the house and where she thought the dope was hidden. You would think with Sally's profession, she would be comfortable being naked in front of a man, but she was quite shy, she tried to cover her important parts as she clumsily got dressed. Poor Sally, she was always the victim.

Ice Capades

To be a good drug cop, Norm had to learn how to play the game. The way the game worked was that when ever you busted someone with drugs, you made an attempt to roll them and turn them into your rat. It was easy bait to take for some if they didn't want to end up in jail.

Sally told Norm about a father and daughter duo she was buying dilaudid from. She said the father, Duke Delaney, was supplying his daughter Denise. She, in turn, was running a shooting gallery from her house. Another one of his rats had told him that Duke was one of the main dilaudid suppliers in the city. According to that source, Duke had befriended a cancer patient who was selling off his excess pills.

Norm put together enough information to obtain search warrants for both Duke and Denise's houses. They searched Denise's house first and seized fifty dilaudid pills, six vials of liquid dilaudid and some weed, all worth about four thousand dollars on the street. With Denise and her boyfriend under lock and key, the squad went outside the city to search Duke's house.

It was a cold and shitty winter day with freezing rain. The Drug Squad pulled into Duke's driveway and the entry team bailed out. Norm stayed dry in the van with his sergeant. The team ran from the gravel driveway onto the cement sidewalk and the Ice Capades began. The freezing rain had literally turned the sidewalk into an ice rink.

Norm's buddy Jesse was first in line, he was carrying the battering ram. He slipped and his feet went up over his head. The ram went flying through the air, nearly taking out Blackjack who was second in line. He ducked and was thrown off balance, going down like a bag of wet cement.

The third guy tried to stop and not run over Jesse and Blackjack; it was like watching a set of dominos fall. They all tried to get up, but they kept falling back down. Their feet were spinning on the ice like Fred Flintstone's in his prehistoric car. Norm and his sergeant remained in the van laughing their asses off, but they had to get out so someone could get to the front door of the house.

The Ice Capades continued for what seemed like an eternity, until the front door opened and Duke Delaney asked, "Can I help you guys?"

Everyone was out of breath and laughing so hard, Jesse barely uttered the words, "Yeah, you're under arrest."

Another thirteen thousand dollars worth of dilaudid and four grand in cash was seized from Duke's house. Thank God he didn't make the team search the whole house to find the pills. The house and garage were huge. He had the pills hidden in one of his sockets, in his tool box. The team might have searched for hours and never found his stash. People like Duke sometimes cooperated like that, upon the threat of having their whole house trashed by the cops. A proper and complete search usually ended up looking like a bomb had gone off in the house.

Norm managed to arrest Duke a couple more times before he finally saw the light and joined the team, becoming a rat himself. Norm now had a pack of rats that were all squealing on each other and the dealers higher up the food chain. Even Sally's boyfriend joined the team; he wasn't a user, but he was trying to guide Sally down the right path. He figured if he ratted out Sally's sources, she'd have nowhere to buy her drugs.

It got complicated and difficult at times when information flowed in from multiple sources. Norm had to learn how to sort and prioritize it all.

Dinner Time

Norm wasn't the only cop in the Drug Squad executing search warrants. He learned the ropes from the veterans in the unit, the pace was unforgiving. It wasn't a good job for family men, they tried, but many struggled with their marriages. The long hours and crazy shifts were not conducive to family life.

Many days were so busy the cops in the unit didn't even have time to eat. Norm had to laugh at one veteran, Banger, who for some reason always planned his raids around dinner time. He soon learned there was a method to his madness.

On one raid, the guy arrested left a half of a dozen, big and juicy cheeseburgers on the barbeque. The team had burgers for dinner. Later, during the guy's interview Banger told the guy he let his dog outside and fed him the burgers.

The guy exclaimed, "Really, you guys are the greatest."

Banger could make a meal out of just about anything. He always volunteered to search the kitchen.

He hollered out once at another raid, "Hey Norm, you want some soup?"

Hungry and curious, Norm went to see Banger in the kitchen. There he was, eating cold mushroom soup right out of the can.

Banger saw Norm looking at him like he had two heads and said, "What? It tastes just like pudding."

Judging by the size of Norm, it didn't look like he missed too many meals. The crazy hours, junk food, and lack of workouts had added several pounds to his once svelte shape. The late-night parties had tamed down over the years, but there were still plenty of victory beers and pizzas after work. The Drug Squad worked very hard, but they played hard too.

The boys in the office thought they'd give Norm a hint one day. He came in and found his desk rigged for special activity.

They had put a work-out bicycle in place of his chair and duct taped his phone to the handle bars. The emergency snack chocolate bars in his drawer were replaced with rice cakes.

Salvation

Sally helped to educate Norm in his new found dilaudid expertise. On one occasion while out on the road with Norm, she needed to *fix* and asked to be dropped off. He was curious and wanted to learn, so he asked Sally if he could watch her fix.

Sally told Norm to wheel through a coffee shop's drive-through where she asked for a cup of hot water, free to everyone including junkies. Norm parked the van and Sally asked for some paper money. She took the dilaudid pill and crushed it in a ten-dollar bill, the raised ink edges help break it down. Then she pulled her *kit* from her purse. It contained a syringe, spoon, rubber hose, and cigarette filter.

Sally dissolved the pill in a spoon of warm water and placed the cigarette filter in it. Then she filled her syringe through the filter and tied off her arm with the hose. She stuck the needle into her vein and pulled back a bit of blood into the syringe *(this ensures no air)*. Sally then injected the dilaudid into her vein. The drug's effect took hold almost immediately, Sally began to mellow, and she spoke with a slight slur. She said it made her feel at peace.

Sally finally got into the methadone maintenance program, and her life slowly came together. The program was new to the city and it was met with some resistance from certain citizen groups, especially the neighbors where the clinic was set up. Norm was offered a spot on a committee which comprised of the doctors and pharmacists who were prescribing, and dispensing the methadone. The committee was a conglomerate of other groups such as the AIDS committee, and the needle exchange program.

At first, Norm didn't believe in a program that freely gave addicts one narcotic to get them off of another at the tax payers expense. But he learned that the program really did work. The addicts were not reliant on committing crimes to support their drug habits. The methadone kept them feeling good, but not actually high and they didn't have the constant addiction cravings. Basically, it let them function normally in society and it kept them off the street.

The committee was having problems convincing the rest of the community that the program worked, so Norm floated an idea at one of the meetings. Sally was interested in helping other people like herself, so she volunteered to help Norm produce an informational training video. She agreed to be on camera and interviewed.

Sally openly talked about how she lost her baby and eventually, her life to drugs. She explained how she had to sell herself to men to supply her daily drug habit. It was not a pretty story. Norm supplied copies of the video to the committee and police so it could be used for police training and public awareness.

Sally kept in touch with Norm on and off over the years. She will probably live on government assistance the rest of her natural life. The last Norm heard, Sally had moved into a better neighborhood, gained some healthy weight, and had taken on a part-time job. She had considered tracking down her abandoned child, but she knew it was better off without her. She told Norm she would always consider him a friend. He tried to drop by her place a few years later, but she had moved away.

Sally openly admitted that if it wasn't for the methadone program, she would be dead. Methadone was her new lease on life.

Sadly, about a year after writing this book Norm saw a local documentary where Sally was interviewed while once again working the street. She had fallen back into her old habits, this time admitting she was addicted to crack. Such is the circle of life.

5

Hanna and Helen

Everyone on the street has nicknames, making it difficult for the police to figure out who is who at times. The cops in the Drug Squad had nicknames too. They were called handles, used to hide their true identities, especially over the police radio. Norm Strom was "Stormin Norman" during his childhood. The name carried over to the police force, then someone in the Drug Squad shortened it to "Storm."

Actually, all Drug Squad talk over the radio was in code: street names, directions, vehicles, and license plates. *Sample radio transmission*: "The B fifty-two and a mouse are six on the view in a blue skate. They're on the inside track with a half a buck in the till, I've got two for shade." Translated it meant: "The black male and female are south on River Road in a blue car, doing fifty km/h in the inside lane, I'm hiding back behind two other cars." It was a whole new language that Norm had to learn after years of using the standard police "ten code" system *(like 10-4)*.

Many people listen to police scanners strictly for entertainment, but criminals use them to monitor the cops in the case they might be in their neighborhood and they had to shut down their operation. Some criminals always seemed to be one step ahead of the drug cops, so they had to juggle different means of communication to level the playing field.

On more than one occasion Norm had to coordinate a surveillance team over the Mountie radio while staying in contact with the city dispatcher over the city radio. Besides juggling the two radios, he kept in touch with his rat by cell phone. It was quite a feat when you consider the fact that he was also driving a car at the time.

The city Drug Squad was small, but it was able to share intelligence information and sometimes resources with other agencies such as the provincial police, Mounties, and border services. Special projects or joint force operations were sometimes be put together to target high level drug dealers or organized crime groups. In the spirit of cooperation, some of these agencies shared personnel; the city traded people with the Mounties and the border folks. This cooperation led to better information sharing and better end results.

Having a good relationship with the border people meant that their frontline officers could target or profile potential drug smugglers acting on information from the police. One night, Norm got a call from the border. They had three females in custody for being in possession of crack cocaine. The city was introduced to crack by American drug dealers from the metropolis directly across the border.

For those who don't know, crack is cocaine that has been purified and cooked into a solid rock form so that it can be smoked. The high is immediate and more intense. It is also highly addictive. A gram of powder cocaine went for eighty to a hundred bucks on the street depending on quality and supply.

For crack dealers, the amazing part of that conversion is that they got five rocks of crack from that one gram of powder. A piece weighing .2 grams went for fifty bucks. If you do the math, it's a very profitable trade.

In this particular case, three young women from the city were returning from the U.S. and they were caught with crack cocaine stuffed in their bras. Hanna, Helen, and Holly were all young girls who had no criminal records or prior contact with the police. Norm explained to the girls individually how the game was played. It was obvious to him that they were being used as drug mules to get the dope across the border. What he really wanted from them was their supplier.

The Fila Boys

Two of the girls saw the light and decided to cooperate so that they might get on with their lives and not have a criminal record. Hanna and Helen told Norm similar stories of how they had met some young American black guys in the city one night at a dance club. This was not unusual since one of the downtown clubs catered to a totally black crowd. Hanna and Helen were lonely white girls who were a tad on the chunky side and apparently a good grab for the Americans Dwayne and Darnell.

The American boys and Canadian girls all got to banging each other. Then the boys asked the girls to carry packages across the border. The boys said they were routinely searched at the border, and that the girls were less likely to get searched. The boys were wrong.

Dwayne and Darnell came over to the city on a regular basis to see their women and to sell crack. Hanna and Helen were aware of it but turned a blind eye to it because they were infatuated with their American men. The boys came across the border with a couple of other homies. They were easy to spot because of their Fila sports attire. They wore hundreds of dollars worth of it, along with lots of gold bling. They became known as "The Fila Boys" to the Drug Squad. There were other guys that were part of the group, but Dwayne and Darnell were the common denominators.

The city Drug Squad had two separate teams working opposite shifts. Norm was told by the opposite team that they had run into the Fila Boys one night on the west side. They said the boys were trying to set up a place to deal. The Drug Squad searched them for crack but came up empty handed. The Fila Boys were then *voluntarily* deported that night, with a warning to never come back to Canada. The cops were given some attitude by one guy with a braided pony tail, his name was Tyrell. Tanker, one of the Drug Squad sergeants, warned Tyrell that if he ever saw him in the city again, he'd cut his balls off.

Good Girls

Even though Hanna and Helen were the best of friends, they couldn't have been more different. Hanna was brought up in a loving, middle class family with strong moral values. Granted she was a big girl, but she was pretty, well-dressed, soft spoken, and intelligent.

Helen on the other hand, was more of a plain Jane who was brought up in a dysfunctional family and lived on government assistance. Where she lacked in intellect, she excelled in street smarts. Both girls had been ignored by the local boys, so they savored the attention that they got from the Fila boys. They really had no idea that they were just being used for sex and as drug mules.

Hanna was very close to her mother and they attended the cop shop together to speak with Norm about the mess that Hanna was in. Mom told him she was not happy about the relationship that Hanna had with Dwayne, but she wanted to be supportive of her daughter. She dropped a bomb on Norm, telling him Hanna was pregnant with Dwayne's child.

Being pregnant would make staying away from, and ratting on Dwayne much more difficult, but Hanna wanted to do the right thing. She decided to stay on the team and to help out in any way she could. Hanna telling Norm when Dwayne was on this side of the border helped, the Drug Squad needed to know where the Fila boys were in order to conduct surveillance on them.

Dance Party

When investigating drug trafficking there are two types of information rats can give the cops: nice to know, and need to know. Hanna gave Norm lots of nice to know information, like full names, descriptions, and even when the Fila Boys were coming to town. Helen on the other hand, gave him need to know information, like where the boys were staying and if they were holding. She knew their street names, who exactly was in town, and usually where they'd set up shop.

It was common practice for crack dealers to set up in a user's house. It put the dealers out of sight, behind closed doors. The host/user would get a commission in dope for supplying the place and their crack head friends as customers. If the dealers couldn't find a private home to work from, they'd set up shop in a hotel room. In both cases, the cops need search warrants to enter and search those places.

The girls both called Norm one day and said the boys were in town. Helen was able to elaborate saying Tyrell was with Dwayne and Darnell, and they were staying at a local hotel. Norm informed his boss who told him to come in early. It wasn't unusual for informants to call him at any hour on any day, whether Norm was working or not.

The boss mustered up enough guys from both teams to work the case. Norm started working on the paperwork required for a search warrant and the rest of the team headed out to the hotel. Management confirmed that the Fila Boys were in a ground floor room.

They supplied the Drug Squad with a room directly across the hall. They set up surveillance on the parking lot entrance to the room, as well as the door inside the hotel. Hotel management was usually very cooperative with the police when they found out what sort of guests were staying with them.

The warrant process takes time, but time seemed to be in Norm's favor since all was reported quiet in the Fila Boys room. Helen called again, telling him that the boys were waiting on the delivery of their crack supply. Hurry up and wait. That was the name of the game in the drug business. Drug time, meant never being on time.

The cops had to sit and wait...and wait. While poor Norm typed his fingers off in the office, the guys doing surveillance in the room napped and watched cartoons. They took turns watching the Fila boys' room through the peep hole in the door. The cops out in the van were jealous when they saw a pizza being delivered to the cops in the room. They had to take turns pissing in a bottle in the cold van, while the guys in the warm room enjoyed pizza and television.

Jesse was one of the lucky ones in the room and he loved pizza. Norm once saw him put away a whole large pizza by himself, with a cheeseburger to warm up. He had been really hungry at the time and the pizza was taking too long, so he ordered the burger to hold him over. Sharing a pizza with Jesse was not a good idea; he used two slices to make a pizza sandwich, and he could inhale four slices to your one.

Norm's fingers were cramped and his stomach growled, but he finished the search warrant and got it signed. He hadn't heard anything from the girls, so he joined the cops in the motel room. Jesse hadn't even saved him a single pizza crust.

A short time later, the action picked up across the hall in the Fila boys' room. They had gotten their crack delivery and were open for business. Jesse gave Norm the room key that the manager had supplied.

The cops out in the van were given the green light and the inside team stacked up in the hallway. Norm quietly opened the door with the key and they all charged into the room. The Fila boys were caught by surprise. Jesse took Darnell out at chest height with a flying tackle, the two of them crashed into the television. Blackjack dove in the air and belly flopped on to Dwayne who was lying on one of the beds. Bongo rammed Tyrell face first into a wall.

Norm let the two cops from the parking lot in through the patio doors so they could join in the action. The room was in chaos…crack and money and bodies flying all over the place. It looked like a shark feeding frenzy. The Fila boys had no time to escape or dump the evidence.

When the dust settled, the room was in shambles. The crack and money were scattered all over the floor, furniture was broken, and there was Fila blood dripping down one of the walls. Tyrell had pulled a knife on Bongo so he shoved his snub-nosed revolver so deep into Tyrell's mouth you could see the outline of the gun in his throat.

He screamed at Tyrell, threatening to kill him.

The Sergeant, Tanker, rescued Tyrell but then asked him, "Do you remember me? I told you I'd cut your balls off if you ever came back here."

He grabbed the knife and started to undo Tyrell's pants.

Tyrell screamed like a baby, "No, please, not my balls…please!"

Tanker then grabbed Tyrell's braided pony tail and sawed it off with the knife.

He tossed the pony tail to the evidence officer and said, "Here, exhibit this."

Norm reached down and picked up a pair of broken sun glasses from the floor, one of the lenses was missing. Darnell was handcuffed, lying face down on one of the beds.

He looked up at Norm and said, "Those are mine."

Norm put the sunglasses on Darnell and exclaimed everyone, "Hey, look at how cool Darnell is."

There was Darnell, looking through the broken sunglasses with a stunned look on his face. Everyone laughed out loud, even the other Fila boys.

He then commented to Dwayne, "Look at you…who said you can't give a nigger a fat lip."

The boys were a bit beaten and bruised, but everyone had a good laugh, until the hotel manager came in and saw the room. The woman looked horrified as she scanned the room from the doorway. Norm later asked Tyrell in the cell block if he regretted coming back to Canada.

Without hesitation Tyrell said, "What you guys did to us was nothing compared to what the cops on our side of the border would've done."

"Sheeit."

Dance Party II

The Fila boys spun through the revolving doors of the justice system and were back in action in no time. A few months later, the girls told Norm that Dwayne and Darnell were now working on their own. Tyrell never did come back to the city. The lure of the women and the easy money that they made from selling crack was just too hard to refuse.

The girls had worked off their charges by that point. Hanna landed a good job and she had the baby. She visited Norm again with her mother, they gave him a bottle of Crown Royal and thanked him for all his help. She didn't have a criminal record to haunt her, but she still had to deal with her baby's criminal father.

Helen needed money, so she decided to stay on the team. Norm signed her up as an official city police informant so she could receive cash for the information she provided. Her personal information was locked in a special vault that was controlled by the officer in charge of the Intelligence Branch. Only he had access to the identities of the individual police informants. The money that the informants received from the police was a joke, but it was money just the same.

The police held auctions a few times a year to sell off unclaimed seized property. The proceeds went into a special fund that informants were paid from. After making a bust, Norm had to submit a written request to the officer in charge of the Investigation Division requesting payment to the informant. He then paid the informant and they'd have to sign a receipt. They were allowed to sign a fictitious name, but it always had to be the same name.

Helen called Norm and told him that Dwayne and Darnell were selling crack from a guy named Rick's house. She even provided the address. It was only a few blocks from Norm's house, on the same street. You just never know what goes on behind the closed doors of your neighbor's house.

Rick was an average, hard working family guy, but he had a crack addiction. He had no criminal record, but his addiction had taken him to the point where he was now letting criminals deal crack from his home. Norm tickled the typewriter keys once again and got a warrant to search Rick's house.

There are basically two different ways to raid a house: by dynamic and stealth entries. The latter is obviously where the cops sneak up, trying not to be detected. When there is a locked door with the unknown waiting behind it, a dynamic entry is required. Locked doors are opened with the master key, a one-man battering ram made of solid steel.

The recon at Rick's revealed that there was a Pit Bull in the residence. A fire extinguisher usually worked quite well on vicious dogs. A spray to their nose sent them running for cover and some never returned.

The plan was put into play with Jesse being the ram man. The Drug Squad quietly surrounded the house and Jesse hit the front door with the ram. The wooden door had a glass window in it and it shattered upon impact. The loud crash scared the dog so badly it puked right there by the door, then ran for cover.

On the way in Bongo shouted, "Hey, remember us?"

The cops charged into the living room and tackled the Fila boys. The boys didn't want to dance like the last time, so they quickly surrendered and submitted. Once again, the boys had to surrender their cash and crack.

While searching the house, Rick's wife came home with a bucket of Kentucky Fried Chicken, Norm's favorite food. Everyone in the house was technically in possession of the crack, so they all were arrested. With no one left in the house, Norm took care of the chicken.

Rick broke down while being interviewed. He said his crack addiction had ruined his life. He was about to lose his house and his job. He said that he was relieved when the cops crashed through his door since he had run out of money and he was about to offer his wife to the Fila boys for sex.

Helen found herself a new black stud and she stayed in touch with Norm for a while. She helped him bust a few more of the Fila boys. They eventually got the message that they weren't welcome north of the border. She got the odd part time job, but her life pretty well remained the same, going nowhere. She was content with that, and the few bucks that she made from being a rat. She eventually stopped calling and Norm never heard from her again.

He always thought that Helen was like the two large turtles that she kept in an aquarium in her living room. Like them, she lived her life from inside the box. Life offered her a few treats for sustenance, but she was content in her environment with no desire to change it.

Norm ran into Hanna a few years later. She was doing well as a single mom and she had a good job. She had finally dumped her Fila boy and got on with her life. Unlike her friend Helen, Hanna was raised to expect more from life. She set her sights on a brighter future somewhere down the road and then she set out after it.

6
Cracker Jack & Ronny the Robber

Jack was a crack head. If you were to look up crack head in the dictionary, you might see Jack's picture there. He was from a poor black family, second generation welfare folks who lived in the city's worst housing projects. The whole family was dysfunctional. Jack supported his drug habit by shoplifting and petty thefts. He would sometimes boost enough groceries to feed his whole family, but he traded the food for dope. Some dealers take cash or trade.

Jack even looked like a crack head, he was skinny with sunken eyes and the trademark rotten teeth. The hot smoke from the crack pipe had deteriorated his voice to the point that he was hard understand him at times.

Cracker Jack was another person who called the Drug Squad one day and Norm answered the phone. There was no mistaking the motivation behind his call, Jack wanted money so he could by crack. He rambled off some familiar names, most of whom were known crack dealers. Unlike the Mounties who gave their informants incentive money for information, the city drug cops needed to see product before payment.

Giving a crack head money in advance of good information was like throwing it out the window. Working with a crack head is something like training a dog, you give him a treat only after he does a trick. Crack addicts will lie, cheat, steal, or even suck cock for their next rock.

The problem with working with Jack was that he only called when he had the itch to get high or he already was. Since getting high was his number one priority, Norm had to learn not to expect too much in the way of reliability from Jack. His information was great, but once he got high, he just disappeared.

One of Jack's regular suppliers was Fat Fiona, well known to the Drug Squad. Fiona was very sly and usually one step ahead of the cops. Sure, she'd been busted before, but she learned from it and she knew how to play the game. She even pretended to supply the Drug Squad with information so they would leave her alone. She ratted out some of her competition or gave nice to know information that never really amounted to much.

Fiona was a single black welfare mom who graduated from the projects, into a special city-owned private home. To her credit, she never dealt drugs from, or kept them in her home. Unlike the majority of other welfare homes, her place was immaculate. She used stash houses or had others hold the crack for her.

She stayed mobile, making deliveries with her car. She'd put the rocks in the back of her mouth, or stuff a baggie up her twat. Crack is not water soluble, so the moist hiding places worked to her advantage. Only desperate crack heads eagerly accepted a rock that had just been inside one of Fat Fiona's dirty holes.

Jack gave Norm information on Fat Fiona a few times, but it never amounted to anything. It was like that with Jack, hit and miss. He tried to set up one of the Fila boys too, but that didn't work out either. Trying to catch crack dealers was tricky, the shit sold faster than cold beer at the ball park. Dealers set up in someone's house with a pile of rocks and then the crack heads flocked there and smoked it all before the Drug Squad had time to react.

Roof Goofs

Surveillance was always a challenge for the Drug Squad. Officers grew their hair dressed down so that they didn't look like cops. Cars were another challenge. It didn't take long for the bad guys to catch on to the particular vehicles that the Drug Squad used.

Sometimes, when the Drug Squad drove through the hood the locals would yell out, "Five-Oh" after recognizing their car.

Parking a shiny new car in the projects made the cops stand out like black jelly beans. On one occasion, Norm was set up doing surveillance in the projects watching a crack dealer whose name and address were provided by Jack. He and his partner Missy watched the house for over an hour, but there was no action. All of a sudden, the target was standing beside Missy's window.

She froze when he asked, "Are you guys' cops?"

"What? Do we look like fucking cops?" Norm barked back. Okay, we're really compensation cops…we're watching those roof goofs over there on that house, there's always one of them faking injuries."

The target returned to his house and Norm discussed his options with his partner. She was sure they had been burned, but then Norm noticed the roofers all packing up and leaving. The word was out, the compensation cops were in the hood.

Roll another One

Cracker Jack finally came through, he delivered up a crack house in the downtown projects where he and his fellow crack heads had been smoking all night. The Drug Squad shut it down, arresting the female prostitute who lived there and her American crack dealer. Jack was completely fucked up that night. At one point, he looked like the silver ball in a pinball machine, bouncing from car to car in the parking lot trying to find Norm. His eyes were like two glass implants and he spoke in broken sentences at a hundred miles an hour. Having completed his mission, he got a cash advance from Norm and was off to the next crack house.

You can never have too many rats if you want to be an effective drug cop. That was the case with Norm, he was always on the look out for new sources. When Jack dropped a dime on a crack dealer in the west side projects, Norm raided his house and arrested the owner with some dope.

Ronny the Robber was a rounder from way back who was selling crack and weed to supplement his government disability income. He was an old, hardcore criminal, doing robberies when Norm was still playing with G.I. Joe's. To his surprise, Ronny rolled over and joined the team. He said he didn't want to be seen with cops in his hood, so he met Norm and Jesse at a local bar. He even bought them a beer.

Ronny looked more like someone's grandfather than a drug dealer. His hard lifestyle had taken its toll, he was sixty but looked seventy-five. He knew everyone and he dropped Fat Fiona's name right off the bat. He said she was a mid-level dealer who was selling to the little guys, like himself.

Norm had only caught Ronny with a few rocks and a little bit of weed so he was surprised that he wanted to work his patch. He was probably afraid of losing his monthly government check. He got to be just like Jack, giving Norm lots of the nice to know, too late, information.

Brotherly Love

Just when Norm thought he had seen it all, Jack called in a tip on another crack dealer, his own brother Jamal. For the price of a fifty-dollar rock, Jack gave Norm all the information he needed to bust Jamal, at their mother's house. So much for brotherly love. They say there is honor among thieves, but there is definitely no honor among crack heads. Ronny never asked, nor ever found out, who ratted him out. He and Jack often gave Norm information on the same dealers. It was all good, having one source to back up the other.

Up Yours

Ronny helped Norm move up the ladder targeting some the mid-level dealers. It was the specific mandate of the city Drug Squad to target street level dealers. Higher level dealers were targeted by special projects by joint force operations between the city and other police forces.

With the help of the customs officers at the border, Norm was able to intercept one of Ronny's American crack dealers. Customs officers made the bust look like it was border related. It took the heat off Ronny, who knew that the dealer was *holding* and coming across the border.

Customs did their due diligence and pulled the dealer over on Norm's information. They found nine rocks of crack in his pocket and other indicia of drug trafficking, a pager and price list. Norm and Jesse got the call to pickup the dealer at customs. Jesse made the formal arrest and searched the guy in the cell block, at the cop shop. Having already found some crack on his person and knowing there was more somewhere, Jesse conducted a strip search.

Norm was collecting the dealer's identification and property when he heard Jesse ask the dealer, "What's that?"

The guy was bent over when Jesse asked, "What is that in your ass?"

The dealer remained silent. Jesse demanded, "Take that out of your ass, or I will."

The guy then pulled a twisted paper lunch bag out of his ass and placed it on the counter. Jesse looked at Norm and said, "You're the exhibit officer, it's all yours."

There were another forty-eight rocks of crack in the bag that had been concealed in his ass. It's a shitty job, but someone has to do it.

The Brady Boys

Being a hardcore west ender, Ronny the Robber knew all the other hardcore families in the hood. He gave Norm information on all three of the Brady boys: Greg, Peter, and Bobby. The boys were part of a dysfunctional west end family. Nobody knew what ever happened to their father and their mother was about at useful as teats on a bull. She was a welfare queen who kept a pig sty for a house.

The kids virtually raised themselves in the tough neighborhood. Basically, they were fucked for life from the moment they were born. There was a girl too, Bobby's twin sister Betty, but she managed to stay off the cops' radar screen.

Norm started with the eldest brother Greg. Ronny said that he was the main weed dealer in the hood and that everyone went to him on check (welfare) day to buy their weed. He pointed out Greg's house to Norm who had a flashback to his uniform days when he responded to a fight call directly across the street from the house.

That house belonged to another crazy west end family. When Norm arrived on the scene there was a bright orange Firebird doing donuts on the front lawn of the house. That was probably a normal everyday occurrence in that neighborhood, but on this occasion, there was a guy wearing only cut-off shorts hanging out of the driver's window.

The car's engine was revving, the loud exhaust pipes were roaring, and the tires were kicking up grass and dirt all over the place. There was crowd on the porch yelling and screaming at each other and at the driver of the car. The guy hanging from the car window had the driver in a head lock. The driver had the steering wheel completely turned to the left so the car kept going in circles as he accelerated, going nowhere.

For a moment Norm considered selling tickets to the circus event. Then the guy hanging on to the driver flew off the car and it raced around the corner, into the high school parking lot. Another police cruiser headed the car off and then Norm boxed it in.

The driver was from a rival clan in the hood and he immediately engaged in a fist fight with the other two cops. One of them pulled out Excalibur and whacked the guy over the head with it until he stopped punching and kicking. Norm was involved in the action at that point, but his right hand got in the path of Excalibur while trying to cuff the guy.

The blow almost broke two of Norm's fingers, he had to wonder how the guy's head must have felt. Everyone broke into laughter later at the cop shop, when the guy stepped up to the registration counter in the cell block. He had been beaten and bloodied.

The guy proudly wore a shirt that read, "Welcome to the city, home of police brutality."

Greg Brady

Ronny told Norm that Greg Brady always had weed to sell from his house, but check day was the best time to raid him when he could have up to a pound on hand. Greg had a lengthy criminal record as well as some biker connections. He was a feared man in the hood, nobody messed with him. Rumor had it that he kept a gun in the house.

Greg looked like and dressed like a dirty old biker, his hair was greasy and always tied back in a pony tail. He had two young children that lived with him. Nobody had any idea what happened to their mother. Like all other dirt bags in the hood, Greg had a big bad ass dog. It was a German shepherd that ran free in the back yard, barking at anyone that came near the fence.

Norm got a search warrant on Ronny's information and raided Greg's house promptly on check day. The Drug Squad found about a pound and a half of weed, mostly divided up into nickel bags, ready for sale. They also found some ammunition for a 12-gage shot gun but couldn't find the gun to go with it.

After arresting Greg, Norm asked where his kids were. He said they were upstairs, but the cop who had cleared it said that he didn't see them. Norm went upstairs and looked in the bathroom. He noticed the shower curtain was drawn closed. He pulled it back and saw Greg's kids hiding face down in the bath tub. He identified himself and asked the kids why they were hiding in the tub.

The older girl said, "Daddy told us to hide here if we ever hear gun shots."

Apparently, the kids had thought the sound of the front door getting smashed in was gunfire.

That tactic saved the boy's life some years later when Greg Brady was shot to death in his own house during a drug deal gone bad. The shooters didn't think anyone else was in the house, but the boy was hiding in the tub like he had been trained to do. Greg had continued to deal drugs right up until that moment of his demise. Norm had busted him twice more before he met his maker.

Peter Brady

Peter was the middle boy and easily the craziest brother. He was probably crazier than he was dangerous. Either way, nobody messed with him either. He too had the biker look, with light brown frizzy hair that he usually tied back in a pony tail. He sported a Colonel Sanders type of beard, minus the moustache.

He lived in jeans, a white wife-beater shirt, and he always wore the trucker-type wallet and chain rig. He lived alone. Ronny said Peter usually had drugs in the house too, but he sold on a smaller scale than Greg, who was probably his supplier.

Norm whipped up another search warrant on Ronny's information and raided Peter's house. As it turned out, Peter was growing his own weed. There were seedlings, marihuana plants, pots, and leaves set out to dry all over the house. One of the drug cops called Norm into the den to show him Peter's collection of newspaper clippings that he had pinned up on the wall.

The clippings were all about the mayor, police chief, and other political figures. He made a point of being a political activist, fighting for causes like the legalization of marihuana. He proudly displayed his threatening letters to city officials in a scrap book. He kept copies of his trespass notice that said that he was barred from city hall.

Norm gave Peter the team speech and explained to him how he could help himself if he wanted to. He knew it was a waste of time, but he did it anyway and gave Peter his business card as he left the house. About a month later, Norm got a call from a traffic cop who wanted to know why his business card was displayed on the windshield of Peter's illegally parked car.

Bobby Brady

Bobby looked like a sickly albino and the runt of the litter. His skin was pale, and he was really skinny. Like his brothers, he favored the long-haired pony tail look and was known as a drug dealer. Bobby also lived alone. Once again, Norm applied for, and was granted, a search warrant acting on Ronny's information.

Raiding Bobby's house was like going shopping at the drug store. He had marihuana, hashish, magic mushrooms, acid, mescaline, opium, and an assortment of legal and illegal pills. He also had a collection of legal and illegal knives…pocket knives, switchblades, daggers, hunting knives, and even a machete. He could have easily opened a booth at a gun and knife show.

Norm didn't hear much about the Brady boys after Greg was murdered, until after he retired. He read in the local newspaper that Bobby had just been sentenced to three years in jail for possessing another assortment of drugs and a sawed off shot gun. Apparently, the family business was still alive, and well.

Austin Grey

Ronny the Robber worked his patch and his charges disappeared. He called Norm from time to time while trying to keep his grandson on the straight and narrow. He was of the silly belief that he could keep him out of trouble by having his dealers arrested. Ronny had proven himself as a reliable informant, so Norm had to give his information serious consideration. That was the case when he reached out to Ronny after being transferred to the B & E Squad.

Norm was working a case where a fellow police officer's home was broken into. His gun and bullet proof vest were stolen. Ronny said he had heard that one of the neighborhood punks was showing off a gun that he had stolen. The kid was also dealing weed, so Norm had enough grounds to obtain a search warrant. Since there was a gun involved, Norm called in the S.W.A.T. team to handle the entry.

The townhouse was in the middle of the west end projects, and it was tough to approach it undetected. A plan was hatched in which the drug guys drove the S.W.A.T. guys there, and then they all bailed out of their vehicles on the roll. It looked just like it does in the movies as the cop convoy came around the corner, then the S.W.A.T. cops in combat fatigues bailed out and rushed the house.

By the time Norm got into the house, all the occupants were hog tied and face down on the basement floor. During a search of the house, the Drug Squad recovered the cop's gun, vest, and some ammunition. They also found a quarter pound of weed. Norm went over to chat with Austin Grey, the kid who had the gun. He was laying face down on the floor near the couch.

When Norm rolled him over, a few of the cops started laughing out loud. Somehow during the take down Austin ended up face first on a huge, pink, rubber dildo. He was a tough kid who didn't seem to care about anything.

His parents were great people, they always wondered where they went wrong. Austin's dad once told Norm he had to take a pellet gun away from him because he was shooting everything and anything in the neighborhood. The kid was just plain bad news. He knew he would run into Austin Grey again.

Solve no Crime before Overtime

The next time Ronny the Robber called Norm, he said that he had been approached by some of his old buddies who were looking to pull a robbery. The guys knew that Ronny was a stand-up guy with big balls, so they wanted him in on the score. Ronny stayed in the loop long enough to supply Norm with all the details, then he told his buddies he couldn't go through with it.

The plan was to rob a local strip bar early in the morning before the owners made their bank deposit. They were going to use guns and jump the janitor when he arrived to clean up in the morning. It had to be done on a weekend when the safe was full of cash.

Norm ran the information up the ladder to his boss, and then his boss' boss. The problem was that nobody in the B & E Squad was scheduled to work on the Saturday or Sunday night when the robbery was to take place. That meant a team of officers would have to be paid overtime to do an overnight stake-out.

Dollars and cents usually outweighed common sense, but the decision makers couldn't take the chance that the robbery would go down and someone might get hurt. It wasn't going to be just a property crime.

Ronny said that the heist was a go, so Norm and his fellow officers staked out the bar for two nights. His boss was his old training officer, Andy Green. He enjoyed the chance to get out of the office and to make some overtime. Nothing ever happened, but all the cops involved got a little extra cash in their Christmas stockings that year.

Ronny called Norm back a couple days before New Years Eve. He knew all kinds of heavy hitters, and for some reason they still included him in their plans. He told Norm that a couple of his buddies were going to take down a biker from out of town who was sitting on two hundred pounds of weed.

The biker club was going to leave just one guy to babysit the stash while the rest of them went out partying for New Years Eve. They knew the biker would be armed, but they were prepared, and quite willing to take him out for the considerable amount of weed they'd get in return.

Andy Green rolled his eyes, but then he smiled when Norm said, "More overtime boss."

The rip off turned out to be out of Norm and the city's jurisdiction, so the information was passed on to the provincial police. They were anxious for more information, but Ronny's wife died and he didn't call back. Norm didn't hear from him until New Years Day. He said the rip-off was postponed, but it was still being planned.

The provincial police lost interest after the information didn't pan out. Someone in the biker gang made a good New Years resolution by deciding to move the load of weed. Ronny's buddies missed their window of opportunity and that was that.

Ronny the Robber was legally a senior citizen and a widower. He turned his attention to his crack head grandson, feeding Norm the odd tidbit of information in the hopes he could help keep the kid away from the wrong sort of people. Old age and grandchildren finally slowed Ronny down. He had some great stories to pass on to his grandchildren. He lived a hard life, but will probably out live Norm.

Some informants come and go like a cold sore, you are never quite sure when one will show up. That was the case with Cracker Jack. It was not unusual; other guys in the Drug Squad had informants like him. The cops use their informants, and the informants use the cops, it's the circle of life in the drug world.

Jack bounced from one crack house to the next in search of his next high and the true meaning of life. Life itself eventually caught up to him and his American cousin on the other side of the border. The two men were unceremoniously gunned down in a dark alley by the police. It was a drug raid that went terribly wrong for Cracker Jack.

A six-line story on page five of the newspaper was his eulogy. It was no surprise to Norm, Jack lived for drugs, so it was only fitting that he died that way. His brother Jamal carried on the family name, one day he beat a guy to death right on the street. He went on to spend his life in jail, where he then killed someone else. Jamal will reside there for the rest of his life.

7
Danny Dugan

During the fifteen years that Norm spent in uniform, he locked up more than his fair share of bad guys. On one particular shift while he was working in Motor Town, he was partnered with a rookie female. On the first cruise up Ford Road, Norm spotted one guy who was wanted for outstanding arrest warrants. While affecting that arrest, he noticed another neighborhood dirt bag that was breaching his parole conditions. Then as he and the paddy wagon drove up the street with their prisoners, Norm spotted yet another wanted person to add to the load.

They hadn't even been on the road an hour yet and the rookie said, "Are you just about done?"

The one thing that frustrated Norm and every other cop was that no matter how fast you locked the bad guys up, the system put them right back on the street. It was not unusual to see a criminal with a three-page record card and thirty percent of the charges listed on it as either withdrawn or dismissed.

The Game

Working in the Drug Squad gave Norm a whole new perspective as to what kind of deals were made behind the scenes and how some charges *disappeared* from record cards. It was the game. A guy got arrested for a criminal charge, and then he would trade information on other criminals or criminal activity in consideration for leniency on his charges.

If the police came up with something good enough, their charges could disappear. That was not always easy to pull off, the trade had to be worthwhile and any deals had to be cleared through the prosecutor if the charges were already laid.

Basically, it's like you see on TV. If you help the cops before you're arraigned on your charges, you have a chance at walking out the door. That is how the game is played and many career criminals are quite aware of it.

One night, Norm got a call from Kirk Westwood, the Detective Sergeant. Westwood was known as the Dirty Harry of the city police force. When he barked, even the brass jumped. He was a legend in his own time. He was known for solving some big murder cases, and the way he took charge of an investigation.

If he got a call for a serious crime he'd stand up and shout across the office out loud, "Nobody's going home!"

Westwood told Norm to grab a notebook and meet him upstairs by the interview room. He met him outside the room and got the scoop. Westwood said the guy inside the room had been arrested for breaching his court-imposed conditions. It was his third offence for the same thing, and he knew he'd be going to jail this time. He told Norm that the guy was a long-time informant of his and that he knew how the game was played.

The deal was that the guy had to give Norm the name of ten separate drug dealers or guys who could be arrested for anything else. That was the trade for his freedom. Norm just about shit when Westwood opened the door and introduced him to Danny Dugan. He had arrested Dugan on at least three prior occasions in Motor Town.

One balmy summer night, Danny and his brother were involved in a shoot out with the neighbors in the alley behind their house that ran parallel to Ford Road. By the time Norm arrived, Danny was sitting on his back porch drinking a cold beer, pretending that nothing had happened. It was like the Hatfield's and McCoy's with the Dugan's and another neighborhood family, the Molnars. The feud had been going on for years. Some said it was over one of Danny's brothers molesting a younger Molnar girl.

Danny pulled out a shot gun and fired it at one of the Molnars while he chased him down the alley. Norm and the other cops searched for hours but couldn't find the shot gun anywhere in the dark alley. Danny sat on his back porch, grinning. Norm felt like he was playing a game of *hot and cold* with Danny. Every time he got near a certain garden shed, Danny would take notice, then look away. They searched it twice, but here was nothing inside except garden stuff.

Norm's partner Digger said he was going to have another look. Norm thought it was time for a different perspective. He went over to Danny's house and climbed up the stairs to chat with him on the back porch. From there, Norm shined his flashlight across the neighbor's yard over to the shed where he saw something shiny on the roof. A smile appeared on Norm's face, he hollered over at Digger to check the shed roof. Digger climbed up the fence and looked on the shed's roof.

He hollered back, "Look what I found, Norm."

He was holding up a long-barreled shot gun.

Norm looked at Danny and said, "I hope you enjoyed that beer, cause you're going to jail."

Danny had a long history with guns. When he was a young boy, he hid up in the attic when his drunken and abusive father chased him through the house, threatening another beating. As the story goes, Danny dropped his father with one shot right between the eyes, when he kicked open the attic door. The shooting was ruled as self-defense.

The Trade

Danny smirked as Norm sat down and placed his notebook on the table in between them. His record card looked like the classified section of the city newspaper. He had been in and out of jail since he was a teenager. He was a tough guy who grew up in a tough neighborhood. The constant beatings from his father probably had something to do with it. He went to the school of hard knocks and was educated on the street. It all made sense then to Norm when he looked at the number of charges that had been stricken from his record card.

Before he could get the cap off his pen Danny said, "Ok, let's get to it so I can get out of here. I need a phone to make some calls to ask around and see what's up."

Norm had a phone brought into the room, and Danny went to work. Danny dialed up guys and asked who was holding or who had what. When someone questioned him, he simply said he was trying to set a deal up or that he wanted to rip them off. He laughed and carried on with the guys on the other end of the phone while Norm played secretary, scribbling names and details in his note book.

Within twenty minutes, he was able to supply Norm with nine separate names of guys who were either were wanted by the law, and/or were holding large amounts of cocaine or marihuana. He knew Danny wasn't bullshitting because the Drug Squad already had investigative files on half the names that he supplied. Norm figured nine out of ten names was a pretty good trade, and the information sounded solid. He gave Westwood the green light to release him.

Danny had proven himself reliable to Westwood in the past so Norm got busy doing follow-up investigation and search warrant preparation. It was a bittersweet relationship for Norm since he'd spent over two years trying to cultivate an informant in Motor Town. Who knew that a man he had arrested before would already be on the team, just with a different coach?

As a result of Danny's information, Norm was able to execute three separate search warrants that led to arrests and large seizures of marihuana in each case. Another guy was arrested for outstanding warrants. Some of the other targets on the list were eventually busted. Danny was considered a hard-core criminal on the street. He was associated to biker gangs.

If anyone knew how he dealt away his charges, the police would have found him laying face down in a shallow grave somewhere. It was a deadly game he played, but he knew exactly how to play it. He never considered himself a rat, just someone working a patch, trying to keep himself out of jail.

Norm ran into Danny a couple more times over his career. He just smiled and nodded to Norm; it was his way of saying hey. He's still out there somewhere. With Kirk Westwood and Norm both being retired, Danny will need a new coach.

8
Special Projects Part 1:
Getting Wired

"A man must know his destiny. If he does not recognize it, then he is lost. By this I mean once, twice, or at the very most three times, fate will reach out and tap a man on the shoulder. If he has the imagination, he will turn around and fate will point out to him what fork in the road he should take. If he has the guts, he will take it."

-General George S. Patton Jr.

Norm loved a challenge…both on and off the job. Sports like bowling, baseball, football, basketball and water polo were challenging. Motorcycle riding, demolition derby, sky diving, and bungee jumping were an adrenaline high. Just becoming a cop was a challenge for him, he didn't know anyone on the job, and he really knew nothing about the job. After high school, he swore he'd never work in a factory. Police work looked much more interesting and challenging

Admittedly, he floundered somewhat in his first half dozen years on the job. Then he caught the seven-year itch and almost quit while contemplating buying a fishing lodge up in northern Ontario. It wasn't until he got a steady partner and worked a steady district that he found a sense of purpose. It was his time to get serious about being a good cop.

Those years in uniform gained him a reputation as a good street cop. He was praised by his colleagues and even the defense attorneys who represented the criminals he locked up. But after fifteen years of working the front line on the street, Norm grew weary and bored. There had to be more.

Only Dopes Sell Dope

After getting a taste of working in plain clothes, Norm spread his wings. He excelled in the Drug Squad and became an expert witness for marihuana, cocaine, and dilaudid trafficking cases. Being an expert meant you could give your opinion while testifying. He had to admit, it was kind of cool when a judge accepted his opinion over the lawyers. If he couldn't dazzle the court with his brilliance, he baffled them with his bullshit.

The city police didn't have any written policies or directives for its officers to do undercover buys at that time. Norm asked his sergeant if he could try to make a buy from a target in one of his files. The guy was reportedly selling crack from his house. All the guy had to do was say no to the stranger at his front door, but greed convinced him to do otherwise.

Norm did a simple door knock, dropped a name, and asked if he could buy some rock. When the guy said he didn't sell that, he asked for some weed instead. He got invited into the house and had to wait in the living room with the dealer's wife while he made a phone call.

Norm tried not to freak-out when the woman said, "You look familiar."

Then she added, "Do you go to the bar down the street? I win the wet t-shirt contest there every weekend."

Norm was disgusted just by looking at the woman's big floppy titties through her sweat shirt, seeing them in the flesh would have made him gag.

The target said he had to go out for a minute, so his wife continued to babble on. She asked if he had heard about the big fight out front of their place where the cops had beat the shit out of one of their friends. Norm's partner Missy asked if she knew who the cops were. Norm saw the puzzled look on the woman's face and cut Missy off.

"Yeah, those fuckin cops, they're all power trippers."

The woman agreed and continued to babble until the dealer returned and sold Norm a nickel bag of weed. His co-workers later arrested the dealer for trafficking.

He was taken to the cop shop and placed in an interview room there. When Norm walked in the guy put his head down and melted into his chair. He said he knew that Norm was a cop, but he needed the money. It really didn't matter; he was going to jail and Norm had made a successful drug buy.

Jesse James

Normally, undercover work was done by out-of-town cops. It made sense, for officer safety reasons. That was easier said than done for street level buys in the city, so Jesse and Norm improvised, sometimes using their own vehicles to make buys.

The Drug Squad cars were heat scores, well-known by too many criminals. The force was tight fisted with its money so they made their own flash roll of counterfeit cash. It was used when trying to make drug buys in the case that the dealer wanted to see the cash first.

Even though Jesse and Norm were the best of friends, they had two completely different styles of policing. Jesse was a cowboy, born a hundred years too late. He loved kicking in doors and pushing the envelope.

There was no doubt that he could handle himself, Norm had seen proof of that way back in their old water polo days during a bench clearing brawl where Jesse took on three guys at one time, in the pool. He wasn't impressed that Norm stayed on the sidelines with the women. In Norm's opinion, Jesse was doing fine and holding his own.

Jesse had a glass heart, but an iron fist. There was one poor bastard who made the mistake of jumping him from behind in an alley one night. Jesse instinctively reached back and pulled the guy over his shoulder. He punched him in the face three times and then handcuffed him.

The kid later complained of police brutality. There *was* no brutality, but the kid's face looked like it had been hit by a baseball bat. Norm was always glad that Jesse was his friend and not his enemy, he was one of the toughest guys that Norm knew.

Ignoring Norm's concern for his personal safety, Jesse set up a weed buy from some unknown dealers, with the aid of a police agent. Jesse used the flash roll to make the buy. The team kept surveillance on him while he drove around the city trying to make the dope connection. They lost sight of Jesse when he pulled in an alley to make the deal. He tried to arrest the guy by himself during the money exchange when the dealer caught on to the fake cash. The fight was on.

It was quite a scene when Norm pulled up, Jesse had the guy pinned to the ground with his knee on his back and a bowie knife to his throat. The police agent was running around trying to collect the fake money that was blowing all over the alley and parking lot. Jesse and Norm were not afraid to break new ground in the pursuit of making drug busts. Besides, it was fun.

Eavesdropping

One day, Norm's boss Teflon Tim asked him to join him in the wire tap room up in the intelligence office. The detectives from the B & E Squad were doing a wire tap on a group of guys responsible for a string of break-ins.

The detective running the investigation asked Norm if he'd be interested in listening to the tapes and reading the transcripts to see if there was any drug talk going on. The civilian monitors transcribing the tapes didn't understand the coded talk that they were listening to, and the B & E detectives didn't have the drug expertise to pick up on it.

After one night of listening to the tapes, Norm was on his way to writing the first drug wire tap to ever be done by the city police. Normally the Mounties handled the drug wire taps from their office.

He wrote what is called a Part VI wire tap authorization allowing him to legally tap ten different telephone lines for a period of ninety days. It had to be approved by the police brass, then read over and signed by a judge. The judge was not impressed that one of the names listed in the authorization was a city cop.

The B & E Squad had suspicions because of Matty Allen's connections to two of their targets. His voice was identified by an Intelligence investigator on some of the taped conversations.

Norm found the wire tap was kind of cool, you got to listen to people's private conversations. One target in particular, Jimmy Smith, was quite hilarious. He'd tell callers not to say anything over the phone because the cops were listening.

Smith said, "Listen, you can hear the tape recorders."

Then he'd openly make a drug deal during the same call. A few calls later, his wife got on the phone with her girlfriend and talked about some other guy she was banging.

The drug investigation took on a life of its own. Norm had to try and identify all the incoming and outgoing calls. With a legal wire tap, the phone company was obliged to supply the owners of the land lines, but cell phones and pagers were becoming more widely used at the time.

Instead of talking on the phone, perspective drug buyers called dealers on their pager, leaving a code that identified them and what they wanted. It was just one more way that drug dealers stayed one step ahead of the cops.

Norm had a buddy at a local telecommunications company. He helped Norm to implement an idea that hadn't been done before. Legal authorization was not required to intercept pagers, so his buddy cloned the pagers that were being serviced through his company. So, in substance Norm had six pagers the same as his targets' that went off whenever they received calls.

Between the tapped phones, and the pagers Norm was better equipped to track the movements of the drug dealers. So that his co-workers weren't disturbed by the beeping pagers, he switched them all to vibrate mode. It was hilarious, one morning he came into work and saw that the pagers had vibrated all over his desk and on to the floor during the night.

By using the intercepted calls as pieces of a puzzle, Norm was able to figure out that there was one main buyer who made regular trips to Montreal and brought large quantities of cocaine back home with him. It was great to acquire such information on paper, but live surveillance and physical arrests had to be made to prove his theories.

As with any organization, the bosses want to see results, patience was not one of their virtues. Human tape monitors cost money, and Norm's big boss wasn't happy about the added cost of manpower.

Making Friends

The problem with him going out and making a bust simply on the wire tap information meant that the whole investigation would be compromised, and essentially over. He identified a splinter group, operating separately from the main targets and he was able to get a search warrant for Jake Lamar's house. Jake and his wife Laura were arrested with cocaine and charged with possession for the purpose of trafficking. Jake was no stranger to the system, he had only four words for Norm:

"Lawyer" and "Go fuck yourself."

Laura, on the other hand, cried like a baby. That is why it is important to interview people separately. Jake was a hard ass, but he had no idea what his wife would say. She was embarrassed and worried about her family finding out. She worked at her family's restaurant, a successful business in the city.

Laura helped connect the dots on Norm's flow chart of names and who was who from the wire tap information. Regardless of what her husband thought, Laura wanted to be on the team and to make her charges go away.

One late night at work, Norm cut through the gym on the way into the locker room. Matty Allen was working out. On the way to the toilet, Norm heard a pager vibrating on a bench in the aisle. He glanced down and took notice of the number displayed on the pager; it was a target's number from the investigation.

The pager belonged to Matty. Norm kept his boss, Teflon Tim in the loop, but he really didn't want to get involved. Norm was uncomfortable with the whole situation because Matty was of the same rank. There should have been a senior ranking officer overseeing the investigation.

Good or Bad?

After only thirty days into the ninety-day authorization, Norm returned from a weekend off to find that his big boss had shut the wire tap down. The senior officer explained to him that is was his belief that the whole investigation was only about *steroids* and not cocaine or marihuana. He said he further believed that the connections to Matty Allen were only coincidental and that he might be using some mild steroids to enhance his workouts. Norm was pissed. His boss Teflon Tim just shrugged it off.

Norm went on a crusade and executed search warrants at the homes of two of the main targets of the investigation. At Jimmy Smith's house, cocaine, a loaded rifle and a loaded hand gun were found. Smith's room mate was caught in the dragnet and became another one of Norm's rats.

At Craig Santos' house, two pounds of weed and a sawed off shot gun were seized. Smith was arrested later that night coming home with even more cocaine and a wad of cash. Norm made a special trip to the big boss' office first thing the next morning and apologized for finding only drugs and guns, but no steroids.

There was one nagging concern for Norm after the wire tap was shut down. What about Matty Allen? He might have to work with the guy some day. Allen could have simply been high school friends with the targets. Then again, maybe there was more to it. He really needed to know if Allen was good, or bad.

One of the legal requirements of a Part VI authorization is that the people whose phones are tapped have to be personally notified of the interception. Allen was brought into the chief's office where he was notified of the wire tap. They asked him directly if he knew Jimmy Smith or Craig Santos. Allen admitted that he knew Santos from high school, but not Smith. They asked if he was involved with or dealing drugs and he said no. That was the extent of the inquiry.

Norm was then called to the chief's office for a project debriefing. The chief told him that Matty Allen denied any wrong doing and that he only knew Craig Santos from school. They hadn't asked him if he knew Smith by his previous surname of Jones. Norm knew that Smith had in fact installed an appliance at Matty's house. It was also Smith's phone that the cop was recorded on while he talked about *funny money*…some kind of coded language.

A sergeant, who was responsible for getting the listings from all the phone numbers that came up on the wires was found to be derelict in his duties and transferred out of the intelligence unit. There were too many coincidences that Norm could not explain, but the investigation was over as far as the powers to be were concerned.

In his own mind, Norm was never sure one way or the other, whether Matty Allen was good or bad. Everyone said he was a good cop on the street, no one could not dispute that fact.

Years later, Jesse James' twenty-one-year-old son died of cancer. It was the first time Norm saw Jesse cry; his glass heart was shattered. It was the day of the funeral and Jesse was a mess. He told Jesse to cowboy up and put his game face on. Then Norm had to put his money where his mouth was and address the congregation with a eulogy.

The room was packed with all of Jesse's family, relatives, cops, and friends. Grief and silence hung heavy in the air; you could have heard a leaf fall from one of the trees outside. The silence was broken by Jesse's grandson who ran by the family seated in the front row. It was a welcome reprieve that earned more than a few chuckles.

At the luncheon, after the service someone approached Jesse and asked him where his brother was. He had chosen not to attend the funeral because *he* thought it would be too emotionally difficult. He and Jesse were like night and day. To answer the question posed to him, Jesse looked around the room and pointed to Norm.

"There's my brother right there."

After the luncheon, Norm brought the leftover food platters to police H.Q. He went in through the main lobby and saw that something was amiss; some uniformed officers were openly crying and others were running around the main office. He put the food down on one of the tables in the report writing room.

He stopped in the staff sergeant's office doorway and asked, "What the hell is going on?"

The staff sergeant said, "Didn't you hear? Matty Allen's been shot."

Norm thought his heart had absorbed enough sorrow for one day, he left the building in shock. He couldn't bring himself to tell Jesse, he would find out eventually on his own.

On the day that Jesse buried his son, Matty Allen was celebrating the birthday of his own son. He was working, but he was on the way home for the birthday party. He stopped at a party store only a few blocks from his home. Upon exiting the store, he saw two youths on the sidewalk, near the road.

Matty's instincts told him that they were up to no good, so he approached them on foot. He was working in plain clothes. He asked the two youths for identification as he approached them and he pulled out his wallet badge to indentify himself.

Instead of his identification, one of the youths pulled out a gun and shot Matty point blank. Instinctively, Matty pulled out his gun to return fire, but something was terribly wrong, he was dying. He collapsed and died on a street corner, in his own neighborhood, with his gun and badge in hand. The two youths fled on foot.

Every cop that was working that day felt like they had a rusty steel spike driven through their hearts. They flooded the area and commenced a city-wide man-hunt. Citizens called in with sightings of the two suspects. The cops finally caught and arrested both suspects. The kid who shot Matty Allen was Austin Grey.

Even though Matty Allen was on the way home for his son's birthday, his instincts steered him to the place he would give up his life. He had interrupted a drug deal. Austin Grey was selling crack, and carrying a gun for protection. Matty Allen made the ultimate sacrifice that day, in the line of duty.

The city was outraged and still mourns to this day. Austin Grey never showed any sign of remorse, he will spend some time in jail, but will one day walk the streets again as a free man. That is the Canadian justice system.

Was Matty Allen good or bad? The question and answer really don't matter now. To his friends, family, co-workers, and the city, Matty Allen is a hero.

Driving School

Norm's wire tap investigation was done, but Jimmy Smith's coke dealing was not. Smith's room mate and Laura Lamar continued feeding Norm information, keeping him in the loop as to Smith's activities. He received a tip one day that Smith was going to his girlfriend's house to pick up two ounces of cocaine that he was delivering elsewhere.

Norm and his partner jumped in the squad's mini-van and headed to the address. They set up surveillance on the house, waiting for Smith to arrive.

Smith showed up at the address riding a red and white crotch rocket. He was only in the house a few minutes, barely enough time for Norm to call for assistance from a uniform patrol car. He made the decision to arrest Smith before he left the driveway and got on to the street. Smith was already on his bike, putting his helmet on when he saw Norm pull in to block the driveway. He didn't even have a chance to stop the van, Smith fired up the bike and took off across the front lawn. His partner radioed in that they were *following* the speeding motorcycle. Legislation regarding police pursuits had changed prohibiting most pursuits, especially if the fleeing vehicle was a motorcycle.

Norm tried to keep up to the speeding bike as Smith accelerated down the side streets. He didn't handle the bike well in the corners, so Norm was almost able to keep up to him. Smith got wise and turned out on to River Road.

He accelerated like a bat out of hell and Norm almost lost sight of him around a bend in the road. Smith got bogged down in traffic, so Norm pulled along side him in an attempt to cut him off. There was still no assistance from uniformed police, so his partner waved his badge out the passenger window, yelling for Smith to stop.

Smith revved the bike's engine and accelerated in an attempt to make a quick u-turn. He was going too fast for the turn, his bike slid out from under him, dragging his left leg on the ground. The bike's rear wheel hit the curb; the momentum allowed Smith to get the bike upright again. He cranked the throttle back and left Norm and his partner in the dust. Sometimes you win, and sometimes you lose. Jimmy Smith won that day.

Weeks later Smith was arrested for the warrant on Norm's dangerous driving charge. He was called into the station to interview Smith. He admitted to nothing, just smirking the whole time he was being questioned. Norm got the last laugh that day though when he noticed Smith was favoring the leg that had been dragged on the pavement.

His smirk disappeared when he was leaving and Norm said, "Take care Jimmy, I hope your leg heals soon.

If you ever want to rob a bank in Canada and make a clean getaway, use a motorcycle. Police are not allowed to pursue motorcycles, in any situation. Norm and his partner were called in to the big boss' office and told they had to report to driver training school. They were verbally chastised for chasing the motorcycle, especially while driving an unmarked van.

Norm couldn't catch Smith with the two ounces of coke that day, but he managed to make his life miserable. The pen *can* be mightier than the sword. A conviction at Smith's trial for dangerous driving meant that he lost his drivers license, and that he wouldn't be able to drive his company vehicle to conduct his business.

It was Norm who smirked leaving the courtroom. He gave Jimmy Smith a farewell nod and flipped him the bird just for good measure.

9
Tommy O'Shea

What you never see on television are cops sitting hunched over, behind their desks trying to catch up on days of paperwork. The pace was fast and furious in the Drug Squad and the cops in the unit were always behind on their paperwork. Search warrants, raids, or drug busts always took precedence, with the paperwork left behind to be done another time.

There were notes, exhibit reports, statements, search warrants, judicial returns, arrest reports, news releases, and court summaries that had to be done properly to keep the bad guys in jail. Temporarily, anyway.

It was one of those quiet, catch up on paperwork days when Tommy O'Shea called Norm. He said he wanted to join the team. He admitted right off that he had a lengthy criminal record for B & E's and thefts. He had done some serious penitentiary time up in northern Ontario. He repented and wanted to give back to society by helping the police. Norm signed him up for the team.

Tommy knew the street, and he knew it wasn't hard to find dope there. Norm met up with him personally and knew right off that he'd fit in. He looked like a biker, He was skinny, with long black hair half way down his back and he was covered in tattoos. He wore a black concert shirt, ripped jeans, and one of those wallets attached to his belt with a chain.

Tommy proudly showed Norm a hidden pouch in his cowboy boot where he concealed a knife *for protection*. Norm explained the difference between the nice to know and need to know types of information required to make drug busts, then sent Tommy on his way.

Different Rats

There are two different types of informants the police can use to obtain information. Police agents are one type. Agents are actually hired by the police to supply information for money, under a written contract. In return, they have to appear in court and testify as to the validity of the information they provided.

Police agents are often used to infiltrate organized crime rings or motor cycle gangs. They can be useful in introducing undercover cops once they have the trust of the organization they have infiltrated. The downside of being a police agent is that they usually have to be moved or relocated later, for their own safety.

The other type of informant is a confidential source, they are completely anonymous, except to the police handler. They have to prove their reliability, but they never have to reveal their identity or testify in court. Cops have to protect their sources and are protected by law in that regard. Judges and lawyers can ask, but a cop does not have to reveal the identity of his source.

Norm saw this put to the test several times, once while he was on the witness stand, testifying at a drug trial. Defense lawyers always tell their clients they will find out who the rat is, and in some cases, they actually charge their clients extra to find out. The informant's identity is *never* put into police reports, lawyers just bullshit their clients to gain their trust and then their money.

Upon cross-examination during one drug trial, the defense counsel asked Norm the question, "I'm going to suggest to you that John Doe was actually your informant?"

Keep in mind there are only two answers to that question: yes and no. The problem for Norm was that the lawyer had the informant's name correct. That was the point where the prosecutor should have gotten off their ass and objected to the question saying it wasn't in the public's best interest for the officer to answer that question. If Norm had said no, he would have committed perjury. If he said yes, it could have meant grave danger to the informant.

He looked over to the judge and said, "I don't think I should be obliged to answer that question, your honor."

The prosecutor finally caught on and got into a discussion with the defense counsel and judge about the dangers of questioning Norm about his informant. The judge agreed that Norm had to protect the identity of his informant and should not have to answer any question.

Blackjack, one of Norm's buddies in the Drug Squad, got the same type of question while he was on the witness stand. That judge didn't like the fact Blackjack wouldn't reveal his source to the court, so he called for a private meeting in his chambers. Blackjack's informant called him during the trial saying he was terrified because the lawyer told his client that he would get the informant's name.

The informant was still close to the accused and got play by play action during the trial. The lawyer and the judge were long time friends who vacationed together in the winter. The high court judge and prominent lawyer pressured Blackjack to reveal the informants name, caring more about the money, than the person's safety.

The rookie prosecutor was intimidated by the judge and veteran lawyer. Even though the judge demanded to know the identity of the informant and threatened Blackjack with contempt of court charges, he stood his ground and protected his informant.

The whole trial was a farce. During the trial, the jury was allowed to hear only *pre-selected* portions of the evidence since they might find it too prejudicial against the accused. Blackjack had informant information that the bad guy would be delivering coke to someone else...on a certain time and date.

The Drug Squad set up surveillance using Blackjack's information and followed the dealer to a corner store where they watched him attempt to complete the drug deal. Norm went after the dealer to catch him with the dope in hand, but he tossed it into the snow near a trash dumpster. After arresting the dealer, he followed the guy's footprints in a foot of fresh snow and found a plastic baggie containing two ounces of cocaine.

At the conclusion of the trial, the judge addressed the jury before they were sent to deliberate. The judge basically called Norm and Blackjack liars because they described the *exact* location of where the dope was found differently. One of them said it was near the N/E corner of the dumpster and the other said the S/E corner, a matter of about six feet.

The judge then added that *he* found it highly unlikely that Norm could have found the bag of dope amongst all the trash surrounding the dumpster. Obviously his missed the part of Norm's testimony where he said there was a foot of fresh snow on the ground and he simply followed the dealer's footprints that lead him to the bag of coke.

The one-two punch was delivered when the jury came back from deliberation. The judge told them he wanted to poll the jury as a group instead of asking them individually if they agreed with the verdict. They all nodded to the verdict of not guilty, but then a female jurist in the front row fainted. The judge ordered that the courtroom be cleared immediately. Norm and Blackjack were standing beside the woman when she came to.

She said, "A couple of us thought he was guilty, but we were bullied into agreeing to get the case over with."

The rookie prosecutor was so upset by the whole trial that he resigned from the federal prosecutor's office. Norm and Blackjack told their boss Teflon Tim, thinking the prosecution should demand a retrial. As usual, Teflon Tim just shrugged and then told them to get over it.

007

Tommy O'Shea told Norm he would do what ever it took to help lock up bad guys, but he hadn't really thought of the ramifications of his actions. Norm only used him as a confidential informant for his own safety. Tommy broke a cardinal rule one day when meeting Norm, he brought his girlfriend along and said she was cool with what he was doing.

Norm knew better. If and when they ever broke up, him being a rat would come back to bite him in the ass. Unfortunately, Norm had to say I told you so when Tommy later got dumped by his woman. Things got nasty during the split and she started blabbing to everyone she knew.

Tommy had his domestic problems, but he had a good job to keep him occupied during the day. He prowled the streets at night, offering up some small time weed and coke dealers to Norm. He really didn't care about the reward money; he liked the action.

He told Norm that he felt like an undercover cop, he got off on playing the role. Tommy led Norm to one house where all five of the guys in the house either had drugs on them, or outstanding arrest warrants. Norm rolled one of those guys and he eventually led him to Joe Anthony, who later turned out to be one of his best informants.

Another problem that drug cops run into is trying to protect their rats when they get into trouble. They want to be anonymous, but as soon as a traffic cop pulls them over, they drop the drug cop's name. It's not too hard for the traffic cop to figure out what's going on. It's a dangerous game, but one that many rats will play to their own advantage.

Busted & Burned

Norm got a call from the cell block sergeant one night. Tommy O'Shea was in custody, and he asked to see Norm. He was apparently defending the honor of his new girlfriend at a local bar and he pulled out his boot knife to defend himself. Tommy didn't hurt anyone, but he got his ass locked up for waving around a knife in the bar. Like all informants, Tommy expected special treatment because he *worked for the police.*

Norm had to explain to him how that was not a well-known fact and that his name was tucked away in a locked cabinet for his own safety. He thought he should have received credit for all the busts that Norm made as a result of his information. He had forgotten about the cash he received as a reward for his information. The prosecutor expected a fair trade of something substantial if he was to offer Tommy leniency on his knife wielding charge.

He got bail like any other criminal does and he got back on the street trying to dig up something for Norm. The exodus of his girlfriend was just the beginning of his troubles. He had a chronic illness that eventually cost him his job. His new girlfriend took him in, but Tommy's physical and mental state deteriorated. He told Norm that he was getting addicted to the pain pills that the doctor had given him. He said he felt like a junkie but he couldn't handle the pain without the pills.

A few years later, Norm picked up the local newspaper and saw that Tommy had made the front page. He was on the outs with his girlfriend and he tried to win her back by causing a scene outside the store she worked at. He caught everyone's attention by walking around with a gas can, pouring gasoline all over himself.

Everyone pleaded with him to put the gas can down, but he continued pouring the gasoline on himself. Before anyone could do anything to stop him, he lit himself on fire.

Tommy was engulfed in flames in a split second. Bystanders tried to put out the fire by using their coats. One of them had a fire extinguisher and he managed to put out the fire. A couple of people received minor burns to their hands from trying to put out the fire. His injuries were critical and he was shipped off to a burn unit out of town. That was the last Norm heard of Tommy O'Shea.

A few years later after Norm retired, he struck up a conversation with a bar maid at a local watering hole. It turns out that she was the sister of a pair of brothers that Norm had chased around and locked up way back in his walking beat days. The woman was a hottie, but unlike her brothers, she had never gotten into trouble.

She mentioned that she never had any luck with men and was on the outs with her current biker boyfriend. As she told her tale of woe Norm's jaw dropped to the bar. She said she was Tommy O'Shea's estranged girlfriend when he set himself on fire.

She was one of those women who liked the bad boy type of guys. Norm couldn't help pointing out to her that she might consider changing her taste in men.

Poor Tommy, he got burned in more ways than one.

10
The Watsons

Squeaky Sally always came through for Norm. She kept him current with new dilaudid dealers as well as the old regulars. Sally had helped him bust Paula Watson on at least three different occasions. Paula had been a long-time user who was banging heroin when Norm was popping zits. She started selling dillies to supply her own habit.

Paula was better looking in her day when she sold her ass on the street to support her heroin habit. Then she learned it was much easier to work from home and to sell pills to make a living.

She had been in the game a long time when Norm finally had his day in court for one of her trafficking charges. She whispered in her lawyer's ear, telling him what questions to ask Norm as he tried to get qualified for the first time as an expert witness. The judge did not qualify Norm as an expert. He had to accept the fact that Paula was simply more of a drug expert than him.

Like Mother, like Father...like Son

Tommy O'Shea had told Norm about a guy named Jeff who was selling weed. He had a gun and was driving around the city, dealing from his red camaro. Norm later received another tip from a uniform cop that the guy was in fact Jeff Watson, son of Paula. Norm did his homework and eventually got a search warrant to kick Jeff's front door in. The Drug Squad found a half pound of weed, and ammunition for a .25calibre hand gun, although the gun itself was not found.

Jeff was a good-looking kid—blonde hair, blue eyes, and well-built. The young girls liked him and his fancy car. Jeff had a huge circle of friends. They all liked to party, but not by sticking needles in their arms like his parents.

Unlike his mom who would never become a rat, Jeff went for the cheese right off the bat and joined the team. He was able to help Norm with some of the bigger pieces of the dilly puzzle he had been working on for over a year. Even though he was dealing weed, his family connections kept him in the loop with the Piccadilly Circus. He was completely estranged from his mom, but he told Norm that his father Mickey was also using dilaudid and selling it to supply his own habit. Some families are in the construction or restaurant business, the Watson's were in the drug business.

Jeff told Norm that he hated his father because his two younger siblings still lived with him and they were exposed to the junkies and all the shit that was going on in Mickey's house. He wasted no time in giving up his father to Norm.

Jeff also confirmed to Norm that Duke Delaney was in fact, one of the main suppliers of dilaudid in the city. Rumor was Duke was buying excess pills from a terminally ill cancer patient. Duke was no dummy, he'd befriend a cancer patient and then offer to help them out financially by buying their excess pills from them. Doctors had no problem over-prescribing serious pain medication to terminal cancer patients. It was a futile attempt in trying to improve their quality of life.

Norm had been batting .500 with Duke, one bust and one dry search warrant, where nothing was found. He had struck out on one attempt when he had the cash but had not yet picked up the pills. Surveillance was always difficult where Duke lived and Norm had to rely on informant information to know when he was holding. There were always users going in and out of his place. He also used some of the women, trading drugs for sex.

Jeff gave Norm an engraved invitation to raid Mickey's house where he'd set up a shooting gallery for his dillyhead friends. They were waiting on a delivery from Duke Delaney.

The Gang's all here

Cops have to consider many factors before breaking down someone's door and rushing into their house. They have to make entry plans that take into account foot traffic in and out of the house, and how to approach it un-detected. In this particular case, there were small children in the house, along with some kind of ankle-biting mutt. Other needle users would be in there along with Mickey. The possibility of weapons is always a big unknown. Surprise is the key. It usually takes about six to eight seconds for people to react and realize what's going on when the cops rush in.

The housing projects where Mickey lived were dimly lit. It is always easier to sneak up on someone in the dark, so that was the plan. The Drug Squad packed itself into a van and waited in the parking lot for the opportune moment to attack Mickey's house.

A taxi pulled into the lot and two guys headed to the front door. Norm gave the go-ahead and the team bailed out, running up behind the two guys as they entered the house. The two guys were knocked to the floor, one of them rolled forward, tumbling down the flight of stairs just inside the door. Norm shouted, "Police, search warrant!"

Drug cops pointing guns ordered everyone in the living room to get down on the floor. Once everyone was cuffed and under control, the cops had to take names and identify everyone that was there. Under the power of the search warrant, everyone in the house is put under arrest for possession of narcotics. Who would actually be charged with what is sorted out later depending on what is found? Norm was pleasantly surprised by all the different people in the house. The gang was all there.

Jeff had been in the house the whole time he was feeding Norm information. Mickey and his dad Brownie were there along with Paula, his estranged ex-wife. Norm had to hold back his smile when he saw Squeaky Sally. Duke Delaney was there with a stripper who had been a former rat of Norm's. There was one other dillyhead that he knew, and the two taxi passengers who were in town from Cornhole, Ontario.

Getting in and getting everyone's attention was the easy part. Searching the house and everyone in it was a major chore. Everyone on the squad had been previously assigned a specific task; they worked as a team. Someone had to record all the names and check to see if they were wanted or had any arrest warrants outstanding.

Other officers had to search the occupants and the house. A female officer was almost always needed to search the females. If the Drug Squad didn't have one on the team, a uniform officer had to be called to the scene.

For some unknown reason, it is always really hot in drug dealers' houses. Perhaps it was because *Welfare* was paying the utility bills. Wearing a bullet proof vest and carrying twenty pounds of police equipment didn't help. The raid on Mickey Watson was in the winter, so the squad was wearing warm clothes.

Throughout the search the heat took its toll, so squad members had to strip down, adding their clothes and equipment to a pile in the stairwell. Mickey kept a pretty clean house, so the cops didn't have to shake cockroaches out of their clothes like in so many other houses they had searched.

Sorting Shit

In being the author of the search warrant, Norm got to interview all the occupants of the house, one by one. By speaking to everyone individually, apart from the others, it took suspicion away from anyone who might give up valuable information. Nobody likes a rat, so everyone in the room had to wonder what, if anything, the others said. There was a lot of bullshit to sort through as everyone told their tale of woe, but Norm managed to get at least one useful tidbit of information from each person.

Mickey was funny, he made it sound like the gang was all there to watch a movie, but no one brought popcorn. Everyone hates a whiner, and Mickey was a big one. He told Norm he wanted to help out, but he never really offered any. That was yet to be seen since Mickey took the rap along with the two guys from Cornhole for the seventy dilaudid pills found during the search of his house.

Squeaky Sally told Norm she was there to score from Mickey. Jeff told Norm that Mickey was waiting for a delivery from someone, he thought it was one of the guys from Cornhole.

Duke put some more of the puzzle together for Norm. His previous trafficking charges were coming to court soon, so he was starting to sweat. Duke went for the cheese. He knew Norm had nothing on him, so why not give up some information on someone else to take the heat off him. He was no dummy. He said he was waiting on a supply from one of the Cornhole guys, but not the two guys who were there. The pills in Mickey's house were only part of the shipment that came down from Cornhole.

Norm worked his magic and one of the Cornhole guys rolled over. He said he was just a runner for two bikers from

Cornhole who stayed in a city motel while he did their deliveries. They knew how lucrative the dilaudid market in the city was and they had obtained the pills so cheaply in Cornhole, that it was worth the trip. The guy added that the bikers were heavy users, and that they might be carrying a gun.

Funny Money

Jeff knew lots of people in different drug circles and one in the funny money business. He told Norm that Moe Maker was growing weed in his house. Moe was famous in Canada for flooding the country with superior quality counterfeit one hundred-dollar bills. He is the reason that stores stopped accepting the large bills from everyone.

Color photocopiers were a wonderful invention, and Moe learned how to take full advantage of them. His secret was using top quality paper and different serial numbers. Others had bypassed some of the bill's security features, but Moe became a master at the art of counterfeiting. The R.C.M.P. still use his name when they refer to his counterfeit one hundred.

Moe had a network of people moving the funny money along the highway from Windsor to Montreal and some in the western provinces. Norm later learned from a niece who was tied into the circle just how lucrative the scam was. Moe sold the bills at twenty or thirty cents on the dollar, depending on how much you bought.

Then they'd go on shopping sprees, hitting large retail malls, using the large bills for each purchase. They pocketed the change. They even had the balls to return some of their purchases for full refunds of real money. They sold their purchases on the black market for fifty cents on the dollar, it was all easy money. Moe eventually got busted, and the

Canadian government soon changed the security features on their paper money.

Jeff's information was good and Norm caught Moe about half way through his harvest of one hundred marihuana plants. He had sold off the first half, but had to take the rap for the remaining crop. He had a real greenhouse set up attached to his house. It was on a dead-end street, not really visible to anyone else.

Moe won himself some bonus charges; he had another photo copier and was playing with some new funny money. He was still on parole for the previous offences, so he was not allowed to have any of the equipment he was in possession of.

Double Agents

Like so many informants, Jeff liked to work both sides of the street. He gave Norm information to work his patch, but also to keep the heat away from him and his own criminal enterprises. He had given up his weed supplier Moe, so he decided to get in on the easy cash from the Piccadilly Circus. He already knew all the players; it was a natural transition to satisfy his greed for easy money.

Squeaky Sally and another source gave Norm Jeff's new address and confirmed the fact that he was now getting supplied directly from the Cornhole guys. Good ole Mickey also made a call for some brownie points, telling Norm the Cornhole guys were in town.

Even though Jeff had been giving Norm valuable information, he was still dealing drugs, and he had to go down. He and his sergeant the Italian Stallion set up surveillance about two blocks from Jeff's house. Norm had been informed that Jeff was waiting on a delivery, so there wasn't enough information to obtain a search warrant on the house. His real goal was to nab the main man from Cornhole.

Surveillance can be long and boring and that day was no exception. Norm and the Stallion just chit-chatted and took turns keeping an eye on the house through a pair of binoculars.

Norm was re-adjusting the binoculars when he exclaimed, "Holy shit!"

He saw two guys sitting in their own car, parked about a half a block ahead of him and the Stallion. They were also looking at Jeff's house with binoculars. He was even more dumfounded when the car's license plate came back registered to Mack Crow.

"What in hell were those guys up to?"

There were only a couple of scenarios that made sense and they both meant that some kind of rip off was about to go down.

Follow the Leader

As Norm and the Stallion pondered their options, a car pulled into Jeff's driveway. The passenger got out, went in to the house, and then returned a minute later. Then the car backed out of the driveway and then Mack Crow followed it down the road.

Norm followed Mack and the other car, while the Stallion called for some uniform assistance. Two cars had to be taken down at the same time. The Stallion coordinated things over the radio while everyone followed each other down the road. All the cop cars converged on the procession and were in place when they stopped for a red light.

The Stallion yelled, "Go! Go! Go!"

Both uniform and plain clothes cars surrounded and boxed in both of the drug dealers' cars. The occupants were ordered out at gunpoint. People sometimes think the police are over zealous when doing things like that, but in that particular situation it was a wise move. Mack Crow and his well-known partner both had loaded hand guns under the front seat. They were obviously going to try and rip off the Cornhole guys.

The passenger of the other car had bottles full of dilaudid pills from a Cornhole doctor, but the prescription was not in his name. The uniform cops also found a hand gun under his seat.

Who knows what would have happened if the cops didn't stop these guys, there could have been a gun fight right there on the street?

Everybody in both cars went to jail, but there was still someone missing. Norm got a warrant for Jeff's house to see just what the Cornhole guys had delivered. A search of his house revealed more of the usual suspects waiting for their fix. Jeff had taken delivery of some dilaudid.

He wasn't at the house, but one of the squad members called Norm with a surprise. They found the missing .25 cal handgun that Jeff had managed to keep hidden since his first bust. Guns and drugs go hand in hand, it's a dangerous game.

Norm learned who the Cornhole doctor was that was supplying the dealers and he filed a complaint with the College of Physicians. It took several more months before they finally forced the old horse doctor into retirement. He was dishing out pain pills like they were candy.

Jeff continued to work for Norm and the Drug Squad. The police department didn't like to keep anyone in the Drug Squad too long, so they transferred Norm to another unit. Jeff was introduced to a new drug cop, who would be his handler.

He was another dumb-ass who thought he could trust his girlfriend so he brought her to the meeting when Norm handed him off. He just shook his head. Jeff's girlfriend had been dealing dilaudid behind his back while he took care of his weed business. Norm had busted them together on one occasion with thirty-eight dilaudid pills. Jeff said he didn't know about her private enterprise or the fact that she was banging one of the Cornhole guys who was supplying her.

He later paid the price for his misplaced trust when she dumped him. She left a long message on another drug dealer's answering machine. The message was heard over and over and passed on to other dealers and users. Norm's not sure what happened to Jeff after that, but he did hear that someone trashed Jeff's fancy car and then set it on fire.

Paula continued to be Paula, living one day at a time, getting high as each day passed by. She continued to sell to a few friends to supply her own habit.

Mickey continued to help Norm for a while, but then he lost track of him after being transferred. Children's Aid stepped in after one of the raids at Mickey's house and took his kids, but as usual, they were obliged to give them back.

Norm later received some accolades when the judge who was hearing the case against the main Cornhole dealer quoted Norm from the expert testimony he had given. The judge rejected the joint submissions put fourth by the crown and defense counsel, and sentenced the guy to three years in penitentiary. It was the stiffest penalty Norm had ever seen doled out for a drug charge.

11
Joe Anthony

After two years in the Drug Squad, Norm was on fire, kicking ass and taking names. With more than a few regular rats, the information highway led straight to him. There were some days when he wrote and executed up to three search warrants. That meant working long and crazy hours, but it also meant overtime dollars.

Making arrests presented new opportunities to cultivate even more informants. He had watched the veterans in amazement when he first got into the Drug Squad. Now it was his turn to shine and keep the unit hopping. The Drug Squad was self-motivated, someone would get a tip, then the unit went into action. All the other cops in the unit had informants too, sometimes the action was non-stop.

Most informants are involved in their own drug sub-culture, each particular drug had its own following. Dilaudid users did not normally use cocaine, and coke users are not normally pot smokers. Drug cops had to be knowledgeable in all the drug subcultures, their informants were the perfect source to obtain that knowledge.

One tip led Norm to a body builder who was selling steroids, another drug sub-culture he had to learn about before building a case and making an arrest. Once again, steroid dealers/users had their own following, mostly body builders from local gyms. Norm busted one guy with over ten grand in steroids but then he learned from an R.C.M.P. expert that the amount was not unusual for a top ranked body builder to use personally while he was in training.

Information from an arrest interview led Norm to a couple guys who were dealing steroids and cocaine. He already had a file on Joe Anthony for dealing coke. The other guy was Benny

Bunko. Norm was still busy chasing some of his targets from the wire tap, but the new information on Anthony and Bunko was good. He already knew where Anthony lived and what kind of car he drove. He didn't know if he kept any drugs in his house, but he knew that he made deliveries with his car.

Any Given Day

Working the day shift in the Drug Squad was normally quiet. The cops sometimes had court appearances, or they spent time catching up on their paperwork. Most drug dealers and users don't start their day until late in the afternoon. By starting their day shift at eight or nine in the morning, the drug cops could get a head start on the bad guys.

In an attempt to clean things up after his drug wire tap, Norm prepared a search warrant for Jake Lamar's house. The Drug Squad raided the house and locked up the Lamar's. It was still early in the day when Norm got the call that Joe Anthony was holding a pile of coke.

Norm had his hands full but was able to send a couple of drug cops out to watch Anthony's house. He gave them instructions to follow Anthony and arrest him in transit since he'd have coke in the car with him. He didn't have enough information to get a warrant for the house at that point.

To complicate matters, he had to try and take down Benny Bunko at the same time so one man wouldn't warn the other. He had enough information for a warrant on Bunko's house, but it took time to put it all down on paper and then get it signed. That meant no lunch again for Norm, not a bad thing considering his weight gain while working in the Drug Squad.

The food Gods were on Norm's side. He had to wait for the warrant to be signed and there just happened to be a sandwich shop in the building. Norm was shoving the mystery sandwich into his pie hole when the cops watching Joe Anthony called. They had taken him down with some coke and a wad of cash on him. They said there was more dope in the trunk.

That meant another search warrant for the car, but it would have to wait, one thing at a time. He finished the sandwich first. The day shift was almost over, but Teflon Tim had called in the afternoon shift early to handle all the action. Norm got Bunko's warrant signed. He got another message from the cops with Anthony, he wanted to talk.

That was a first. Nobody ever rolled over before they were interviewed and given the team speech.

Norm had the cops impound Anthony's car until a warrant could be obtained for it, and he had them put Anthony on ice until he could catch his breath. Then he put another plan into place.

The afternoon shift was sent out to play, they hit Bunko's place around 4pm. During the search of Bunko's house, they recovered two hand guns and two rifles, along with some ammunition, steroids, weigh scales, and cut for cocaine. He was charged with multiple weapons charges.

Joe Anthony's car was eventually searched and they found more cocaine and cash in a safe box in the trunk of his car. In total, Anthony had almost an ounce of coke and over eight thousand dollars in cash on him and in his car. Norm noticed a safety deposit box key on his key ring and told him he was getting a search warrant for the bank box.

Anthony confessed that there was another ten grand in the bank box.

Say it ain't so Joe

When Norm walked into the interview room, Anthony looked relieved. He said to Norm, "It's like you just took a piano off my back."

Norm replied, "What do you mean by that?"

Anthony said he'd been dealing for a long time. He was tired of looking over his shoulder, and he had been paranoid about getting caught.

"It's over now" he said.

"What do I have to do to walk away from this?"

There it was, the million-dollar question. He was no dummy, he knew the gig was up and he did not want to go to jail.

Norm explained exactly how he'd have to play the game…how he'd have to give up three other drug dealers or three times the product that he had been caught with.

He didn't bat an eye.

"I can do that."

"Who do you know and what can you do for me?"

"I know lots of people."

Norm leaned back in his chair and listened intently as Anthony talked about the dealers, he bought coke from and other guys that he knew who were selling coke. He talked like a professional businessman, he knew the coke business, no doubt. He was confident and well-spoken, not like any of Norm's other informants. He was clean cut and well built, his body building efforts showed through his designer clothes. His tanned skin and blue eyes were accented by the heavy gold jewelry he wore.

Anthony knew some important people, he either bought coke from them, or sold it to them. He didn't reveal his client list but he said that a former mayor and a prominent city lawyer were on that list. He said he normally got his cocaine from well-known city businessman Michael Cook, who was known for his local charity work. Norm had heard rumors about Cook before, but never had enough proof to start a file on him.

Anthony said he'd buy up to two ounces of coke at a time from Cook or his drug dealer/partner. Cook would never actually touch the coke or money in his presence, but he was always in the room or nearby. He'd broker the deal, keeping a low profile during the exchange.

Playing the Game

Norm was impressed. Anthony said he couldn't give up Cook right off, because he'd know who ratted him out. Cook was associated to a local biker gang and Anthony feared for his life. He would help him to understand Cook's network but he couldn't give him up directly.

The conversation had been mostly one-sided, but then Anthony said, "So what can you do for me?"

Norm told him if he could deliver everything that he promised, he might be able to walk away from his drug charges. The only catch was, once charges were laid the prosecutor would have to be told of his cooperation before the charges could be dismissed. A look of pain started to come over Anthony's face.

"If you charge me, everyone will know and I will be of no use to you."

He told Norm that Cook knew people in the court house and that they always checked the dockets to see who'd been arrested. If the word got out that he was busted, everyone on the street would avoid him like the plague. Norm got the point. If he wasn't left in the game, he wouldn't be able to fulfill his obligations. The situation got into an area above Norm's pay grade, so he went to see Teflon Tim.

Norm explained to Tim that he thought he had a good fish on the line who could lure in bigger fish, maybe even Michael Cook. Tim was impressed and he suggested they hold off on processing Anthony. His charges could be laid at a later date. He told Norm to put him on a short leash, giving him a month to work his patch, in an attempt to make his charges disappear. Norm had been burned by informants with big promises before, but he agreed it was a good idea.

He went back to Anthony with the plan. He told him that they would leave him in the game, but he only had a month to produce results if he wanted to walk away from his charges. He looked like he'd just won the lottery. As a consolation prize, he pushed the envelope and asked Norm for his car, cell phone, and pager back. Tim agreed that he would need those things to play the game, but the cops got to keep his dope and cash as collateral.

The deal was made and Joe Anthony was drafted by the blue team. It had been a very long day, but Norm was sure he had cultivated a very important source.

Cocaine 101

The first thing that made an impression on Norm when he later met up with Anthony was his punctuality. Drug dealers or buyers, or anyone else involved in the business, were never on time. The cops called it *drug time*. Norm met him and discussed some of his options for cleaning his slate.

He had a minor criminal record from many years' prior for a petty crime, but for the most part he had stayed under the radar. He told Norm things about his personal life and how he got into the drug business. He had a family, but he kept the drug business completely away from them. Anthony was serious about his personal health and he didn't do drugs, with the exception of smoking the odd joint. He never used the coke that he sold and he rarely drank. He was a rare breed as drug dealers go, a businessman to say the least.

Anthony had a list of regulars who were long time customers. He did not sell to kids or anyone that he did not know. Most of his customers were loyal. That kept him in the money and under the radar. But in his case, someone got busted and dropped his name. He asked Norm about that, but he didn't push the issue when Norm said that he couldn't discuss any of his other sources.

As Anthony talked about his coke business, Norm listened and learned. Most of his drug arrests had involved dilaudid or marihuana, with the exception of a few smaller coke busts. Anthony explained how dealing in small quantities made him more money and it helped keep him under the radar.

Cocaine is like any other commodity really, if you buy it in bulk, it is cheaper. The coke gets cut as it passes down the supply chain, that adds to the profit margin. He called it his bread and butter.

Hot Potato

It only took Anthony one week to offer up his first fish. He told Norm he'd be meeting a guy who wanted to buy some coke from him. Roger Danby was a nobody, with no criminal record, but he was about to become a somebody. It really didn't matter to Norm who he was. If he was holding the hot potato, he was going to jail.

There are three elements to being in possession: knowledge, consent, and control. When someone knows they're buying cocaine, they consent to buy it and then they take control, or they have *possession*. It is as simple as that. Anthony met up with Danby, sold him the coke, and then let the Drug Squad take him down. Call it a set up if you want, that's exactly what it was.

Of course, in reality, things can't be done that simply. It would have been obvious to Danby that he was set up. Anthony and Norm had hatched a plan where Norm watched the exchange and then the team stop both men as they left in their separate vehicles. After surrounding Danby and arresting him, Norm pretended to shout orders over the radio for someone to stop the guy in the other car.

He then played the heavy with Danby, demanding to know who the other guy was. The trick was to try and take the heat off Anthony, to keep Danby's head spinning and guessing as to what really went down. Teflon Tim was there for the take down. His smile said it all when he found three ounces of coke in the back seat of Danby's car. He saw that Anthony was serious about working his patch and being on the team.

Timing is everything

It was obvious to Norm that Anthony could supply the *need-to-know* type of information. He told Norm about other dealers that he was aware of. Norm's ultimate goal was Michael Cook's organization, but that wouldn't be easy. In the mean time, Anthony offered up another small fish. The bust netted one bad guy, a small amount of coke and just under a thousand bucks in cash.

There was supposed to be two more ounces of coke, but the cops couldn't find it. Proceeds of crime legislation had recently been passed, so if the cops could prove a dealer was trafficking, or in possession for the purpose of trafficking, the government could seize any cash or property believed to be derived from the criminal enterprise. Anthony called Norm back after the bust. He said the guy had a couple ounces of coke stashed in his car, but it wasn't there at the time of the raid.

He attempted to set up another guy that was a well-known dirt bag to the city police. He delivered an 8-ball to the guy, then the Drug Squad followed him and took him down. The guy swore up and down that he didn't have any drugs on him. Norm's partner Blackjack stripped the guy down to his birthday suit in the back of the van, but no drugs were found. They had to let the dirt bag go.

Blackjack was frustrated and said to Norm, "I looked everywhere but down his fucking throat."

They looked at each other and realized that his mouth was the only place he could have concealed the paper deck. A call from Anthony later confirmed their theory. The guy was freaking out during the whole search thinking the coke was going to dissolve in his mouth.

The icing on the cocaine cake was delivered to Norm by Anthony in the form of Drew Dancer. He gave Norm enough information to hit Dancer's house with a search warrant. Norm hit the mother load, Dancer was sitting on over half a pound of coke, worth about forty grand on the street. He also had an illegal switchblade knife.

Anthony had told Norm that Dancer was one of Michael Cook's mules, and that the coke belonged to him. Dancer knew exactly who Norm was trying to catch, but he said he couldn't offer up any names if he wanted to stay alive. His lawyer begged for leniency by telling Norm that her client wanted to cooperate, but he couldn't give up any names. Too bad, so sad. Dancer did two years in jail for Michael Cook.

Norm heard later that Cook asked Dancer for the money he owed for the coke when he got out of jail. His two years in the slammer didn't knock a penny off the drug debt. So much for loyalty.

Joe Anthony did it, he had successfully worked his patch and Norm shredded his whole charge file.

Payback is a Bitch

Life was good with the cops off his back and his business back on track. Unfortunately for Anthony, Dancer had told Cook that he believed it was him was who ratted him out. Not a word was said to him, but one night someone threw Molotov cocktails at his house and car. He was lucky, neither device caused any serious damage.

Cook later verbally accused him of being the rat, even though he had no actual proof. The sad fact is, they really didn't need any proof, the accusation is all that was necessary. It was enough to get him punched in the head one night in a bar by one of Cook's cronies. He suffered a broken nose from the sucker shot.

Maybe Anthony's good luck had changed. He told Norm that someone at his gym stole all his jewelry from his locker, about eight thousand dollars worth of gold. He was not a violent man, and he wouldn't carry a gun like many other drug dealers. He just wrote off his delinquent customers after they ran up huge debts and couldn't pay. He said it was the cost of doing business.

He had one biker customer who placed an order and then pulled a knife when he arrived at his house. The biker wanted his money and his dope. What goes around, comes around though, as they say. Jesse James raided the biker's house at the end of that summer, seizing several towering marihuana plants that he had growing around his built-in pool in the back yard.

Jesse crashed through the front door so hard he literally scared the shit out of the biker's wife. She was in the bathtub at the time. When the cops checked the bathroom, they found her in the tub with an O'Henry bar floating beside her.

Things started changing in the city and across the country as the bikers took over the cocaine trade. They recruited and expanded their ranks, sending out the message, *if you want to deal coke; you'd better deal for them.* Anthony's suppliers started drying up, but he didn't want to deal with the bikers. A buddy set up a deal with an unknown source for him to buy a kilo of coke.

He trusted his buddy and he met him and the supplier at a local motel. The unknown guy introduced himself by pulling out a pistol and pointing it at his head. He tied Anthony and his buddy up, then asked where the thirty-five grand was. It was a rip off. Luckily, he had stashed the cash before he got to the motel. The guy pistol whipped him when he refused to give it up.

Anthony saw his life flashing by as he felt the warmth of his own blood running down the side of his face and neck. The guy threatened to kill him, but he never gave it up. Eventually, the guy became frustrated and took off, leaving him and his buddy hog tied in the hotel room.

He was able to reach a pocket knife he had hidden and he cut himself free. He looked at his buddy before cutting him loose, he wondered if he was in on the whole thing. Once again, he chalked the whole experience up to the cost of doing business.

What else could he do, call the cops and tell them that he was pistol whipped when he wouldn't give up his drug money?

That was Joe's life as a drug dealer and he accepted it.

Cokeheads

Anthony and Norm met on a regular basis to catch up. He wasn't like any other drug dealer or informant. As Norm learned more about the cocaine trade, Anthony learned more about how the cops and the legal system worked. By staying in touch, he figured he got to stay in business.

He kept Norm well-informed but he'd also call for the odd favor, like the time he got stopped for speeding. He called Norm on his cell phone and then handed it to the traffic cop when he came up to the car window. That was the typical cop/rat relationship, they tried to scratch each other's back.

Although cops and their informants developed a rapport, there was a line that wasn't to be crossed. Informants were just that. They were not a friend or someone you socialized with in public. It was a professional relationship and their identity had to remain secret. As much as they liked or respected each other, it was always just a business relationship.

Norm was always interested in Anthony's customer list. He had lots of stories related to his business. After getting pistol whipped, he went out west to visit a buddy, his new coke connection. His buddy was affiliated with a five-star hotel there. He asked Joe to deliver an ounce of coke there for him.

Anthony obliged thinking nothing of it, until a famous movie star answered the door and invited him in. The movie star told him he'd appreciate some discretion. He recognized the movie star and his wife and assured them that they shouldn't worry. They're still married and making movies to this day.

Anthony talked some more about the prominent city lawyer who often called him over to supply his party guests. One night, he said a few lawyers, a biker and a few strippers were at the house. Everyone was fucked up when he arrived.

They were arguing over what to do about one of the guests who was shot in the foot by the biker. Norm found the story fascinating; he had been questioned by that particular lawyer in court on several occasions. He was one of the city's top lawyers who handled many high-profile cases.

The Elusive Mr. Cook

Norm never lost interest in Michael Cook. He paid for his business degree by selling cocaine and he had friends in high places. Anthony provided Norm with the name of another one of Cook's mules who was running cash up north from the city and cocaine back down to the city.

Norm was also getting information from Syd, another coke dealer he had busted on the far west side of the city. Syd was buying his coke from Cook's group. He supplied Norm with some of the same names that Anthony did. Before being busted by Norm, Drew Dancer had delivered coke to Syd on more than one occasion.

Norm put the mobile surveillance team on the mule, but they didn't come up with anything useful. Acting on his direction, they followed the mule to Hogtown. Norm called the drug cops in Hogtown but they said a kilo was small potatoes to them. They said they really didn't have the time to look into it.

He didn't give up and talked the provincial police into stopping the mule on the way back to the city. The kid still had thirty-five thousand in cash, but no cocaine. Norm later heard a couple of different stories as to why the kid never picked up the cocaine. The cops couldn't arrest him just for carrying a wad of cash, so they had to let him go.

Syd was able to meet Cook's coke partner face to face. Gary Norris had organized criminal connections across the province. He was tied into some legitimate businesses, so they could launder his drug money. Norm was frustrated but Cook and Norris were out of reach for the city Drug Squad. They were dealing at levels beyond the street team's mandate. He had to settle for the little fish in the big drug pond.

Doing the Laundry

Joe Anthony continued to supply Norm with good information that led to more arrests and drug seizures. At the same time, his own coke business flourished. He said the hardest part about making all that money was how to *launder* it. Laundering money is the process of making *drug* money look legitimate. It can be done in many ways. It has to be done if a drug dealer wants people to believe that his money comes from a legitimate source.

At one point, Anthony figured his cocaine-fueled net worth was about three hundred thousand dollars. He said paying cash for everything isn't all it's cracked up to be, he got strange looks when he dumped thirty grand in cash down on a new car. Buying a house proved even more difficult, who pays cash for a house? He used different laundering methods, like buying and cashing in chips at the casino. He had to be careful because they monitored large transactions for exactly that reason.

Anthony didn't have a legitimate job, but he decided to claim some income from his criminal enterprise to keep the government off his back. They have confidentiality rules that keep them from disclosing anyone's source of income, so he became a tax payer. He hadn't filed a return for years.

He gave a buddy who owned a construction company a wad of cash for a company issued pay check and tax receipt. It made him look legitimately employed. The heavy flow of drug money eventually forced him to invest in a business with a couple employees. Having a business was an excellent way to launder his drug money. Life seemed pretty good, considering he was a drug dealer.

Women!

After Norm moved on from the Drug Squad, Anthony hooked up with Jesse James, just to keep his union card. Jesse called Norm one day and said that Anthony got busted by the provincial police. He knew exactly how the game was played and told the cops that he wanted to work his patch. They didn't get much when they busted him, so it didn't take much for him to get out from under their thumbs.

Getting busted was the least of his problems. He hooked up with a new woman and was in the process of building himself a new house when she got involved in the design. Out of generosity, he set her up with her own business. He soaked most of his fortune into the castle they built.

One would think that a business to call her own and a new castle would be enough for a woman, but Laura wanted more and started sucking his profits up her nose. She preferred the coke over work and she walked away from her business.

Anthony had no choice but to carry on the coke business. He eventually made the fatal mistake of using his own product to try and teach his wife a lesson. It was the beginning of a downward spiral that lasted over two years. He got to the point where he fell into a deep depression and he physically couldn't get off the couch. The bills stacked up. Laura cleaned up her act enough to get out and pick up the some of the slack, she started doing his deliveries and handling his coke business.

Laura ran the business for some time. He finally came to the realization one day that he'd have to leave town to dry out.

He made the decision to go and see his buddy out west and dry himself out. Anthony was tired of the coke business. He thought he'd invest some money in a grow-op out west, then get himself a job with his buddy, in construction. He sent coke cross-country to Laura, who kept up the family business. Laura's independence, and the past strain of their relationship, gave him the idea he would be better off staying out west.

Norm hadn't heard from Anthony in a long time, but he called one day and said that Laura got busted. She had coke on her and the provincial cops found more in the house. He called and asked Norm for some advice since he wasn't involved locally and he hadn't been living in the city in quite a while.

He may have been a drug dealer, but he was a chivalrous man; he came back home to see how he could help Laura. He would have been better off staying out west. Laura got pissed, left the house, and then filed a police report saying that he had assaulted her three years earlier. It was a ploy by Laura and her lawyer to make him look like the worst offender so he would take the fall on the drug charges.

Anthony was already in a financial tail spin and the real estate market across the country was in the dumps. He had a fire sale, selling his classic motorcycles and his other toys. He turned in the keys to the fancy car he was leasing and he listed his castle for sale. Norm offered all the advice he could, but he was really all alone, awaiting the outcome of his court case.

He had no real friends. He tried to pick up his coke business again and started to get himself back into physical shape. He started to sell his product instead of using it himself. Although he took a huge loss, his house eventually sold. He tried to do the right thing again and gave Laura more than her fair share.

Just when Norm got to thinking that maybe Anthony was getting on with his life, he got a call that he had been busted for causing property damage to Laura's house. To make matters worse, he tried running from the cops and he smashed up his car.

Norm was puzzled. Some time later he ran into him at the gym, he said he plead guilty to the property damage and did the time, just to get it over with. Norm shook his head; he couldn't bring himself to ask him why.

Looking at Anthony, he could see that life was finally catching up to him. His blue eyes were glassy and bloodshot from the joint that he had just smoked. His hair had thinned, it had receded and was mostly grey. Physically, he looked like he was back in shape, but the drama in his life had taken its toll. His permanent smile and charismatic personality were long lost.

Anthony said he now enjoyed his dog's company better than any woman. Norm finally asked him why on earth he went out of his way to trash his wife's place. He had always said he wanted to get as far away from her as possible.

He said to Norm, "It was like therapy."

Norm still runs into him at the gym. One day he told him about his time in jail, about a month and a half of the longest time he'd spent on earth. He said the jail was filled with young men who don't give a shit about anyone or anything. They bragged about how they couldn't wait to get out so they could get back to things like stealing cars and smoking crack.

Anthony was the jail hero when he arrived because he had hooped some weed and tobacco before going inside. The smokers thought he was pretty cool, but a couple of other thugs disagreed and kicked the shit out of him one day for something to do. He is no wimp, but he said he could not relax the whole time he was in there; he was always looking over his shoulder.

He found it ironic how most of the jail population acted like they were on vacation at an all-inclusive resort. Norm recalled interviewing dirt bags who called it the *County Hilton* instead of the county jail. They didn't mind being sent to jail because all their friends were there, it was like a family reunion for some of them.

And so, life goes on for Joe Anthony. He has no real job, friends, pension, or any light at the end of the tunnel. He is a drug dealer, that is what he does.

12
Special Projects Part 2:
Sting Operations

"The pessimist complains about the wind;
The optimist expects it to change;
The realist adjusts the sails."

-William Arthur Ward

As with all good things, Norm's time in the Drug Squad came to an end and he was transferred to the Morality unit. His transfer there was a step up the promotional ladder, but it offered a whole new set of challenges. The unit was responsible for enforcing the liquor laws in the bars, prostitution, gambling, and sex crimes. The transfer also meant Norm had to get a hair cut new clothes, no more jeans. It was a suit and tie office; it was a good thing that he had saved up some overtime cash.

Finding a Niche

One of his duties in Morality was to make regular visits to the bars, checking to see if they were meeting the obligations of their liquor licenses. In his opinion, Ontario's liquor laws were, and still are, archaic in comparison to other more liberal countries.

But laws have to be enforced and someone has to enforce those laws. Working the bar detail on the afternoon shift meant that you got to dress down a bit, no jacket or tie. The object was to blend into the crowd and not be recognized as cops, in the hope you might catch the bar staff breaking the law.

Norm saw that most of the Morality cops were recognized as soon as they walked into the bar. His experience in the Drug Squad obviously paid off since the bar staff was surprised on more than one occasion, when he identified himself as a cop. The only good thing about doing the bar checks was that you got to have a few drinks free, on the company.

Chasing prostitutes was a couple notches up on the fun meter. You cruised the areas they hung out in and then set up surveillance once you saw them in action. An added difficulty for Norm chasing the prostitutes was that some of them were his former drug rats. He caught one of his rats, Mary, in an alley one night with her head buried in a John's lap. The John freaked when he saw the flashlight shining into his car.

Mary just smiled, rolled down the window and said, "Hey Storm, what's up?"

Norm was with his sergeant, so he had to write Mary up for solicitation. In reality, the ticket became motivation for Mary to call him back, she'd have to trade some good information to make the ticket go away. The sergeant wasn't too happy with that, but he knew it's what made the world turn.

The Morality unit also did *John sweeps*, where they'd put an undercover female cop on the street posing as a prostitute. It was like shooting fish in a barrel as traffic backed up with guys trying to pick up the fresh meat on the street. The female cops had to really dress down, most were too attractive to be on the street.

Norm even got to go to *John school* to learn all about a new type of sting. The rationale was that if you kept the Johns off the street, you'd keep the hookers off the street at the same time. The sweeps were no big deal to him, until he had to arrest one of his old high school football coaches. He said he didn't see the harm in stopping for a blow-job on the way home from getting groceries.

Norm needed to find a niche somewhere in Morality, he didn't enjoy picking on the bars or the hookers. The city had just passed a new bylaw allowing licensed escorts to advertise and work their trade behind closed doors. The city had also opened a casino, and the escort industry took off overnight.

The escorts had to register with the city and pay a license fee if they wanted to legally work in the city. Files containing the escort's private information were kept in the Morality office. They had to get photographed and have a police clearance to be licensed.

Norm had difficulty trying to find something in the escort file drawers one day; he took note of the mess and how no one was monitoring anything. One woman had used a fake name and other complaints of non-compliance were coming in to the office. He got an idea and ran it by his boss; he asked to be put in charge of the escorts so that they could be properly monitored.

He also ran an idea by the boss for a sting operation that would surely result in some charges, therefore making the boss look good, he was an easy sell. It was a way for Norm to opt out of the other Morality crap, and to perhaps cultivate a few more informants.

Sex Stings

Norm got friendly with the ladies who worked in the city licensing office and re-organized all the escort files. There were over a hundred of them in the beginning. Putting a sting operation together didn't take too much thought. The law prohibited the escorts from working out of their own homes, it was considered *operating a bawdy house*. For their own safety, they requested a name and landline phone number to make an appointment.

The women wouldn't discuss sex on the phone but openly told clients the cost was a hundred and thirty bucks for the first hour of their visit. Any other arrangements had to be made in person once the escort arrived.

Norm ran the sting a couple nights using a hotel room the first night and the party room of a buddy's apartment building the second. All it took was a bunch of phone calls, making appointments with the escorts about a half hour apart from each other.

Some of his co-workers got in on the fun by ordering up their own escorts. He even called a male escort; he didn't want it to seem like he was just picking on the women. They usually arrived by taxi or had a hired driver/security man drop them off and wait outside. One of the drivers questioned was actually an escort's husband. How weird is that?

Did he ask, "Hi honey how was work tonight?"

The escorts showed up for their appointments one by one, only to be pissed off or disappointed when they found the cops waiting instead of their Johns. They also had to produce their escort license on demand. A few of the girls thought the sting was a good idea because there were a lot of *freelancers* in the trade who were not licensed. They just wanted a fair playing field.

Norm got quite an education in just a few nights; the women were very interesting to talk to. The woman with the husband driver also had five kids at home. She said her husband appreciated the fact that she brought in more money in a week than he could in a month.

The women said that the Johns were from all walks of life. Granted most of their calls were for sex, but there were some guys who were lonely and just wanted to talk. Others were from out of town and needed a date for the night.

The boss was happy, the escorts were mostly happy, and Norm was happy. Within a few days, some of the escorts started calling him to rat out other prostitutes who weren't complying with the bylaw or who were selling drugs, right up his alley.

The escort industry grew like a wildfire and the city made a killing on the licensing fees. Some people started their own escort companies, hiring escorts to work for them. The phone book yellow pages were soon flooded with huge ads for escort services. Between the casino, the escorts, and the abundance of strip bars, the city gained a reputation as the *Tijuana of the North*.

Fixing the Broken Wheel

Another part of Norm's job in Morality was investigating sexual assaults. The child abuse cases were the worst. Norm didn't have any kids, but it didn't stop him from wanting to cut a guy's balls off after hearing the details of an abuse. It was always difficult to listen to two completely different sides of a story and then try to make an informed decision that would affect someone's life forever.

One young girl and her mother had Norm convinced her boyfriend had raped her, until he heard his side of the story. He doubted the girl's version, but had to arrest the boy on the word of the girl. She eventually recanted the day after he put her boyfriend in jail. She said she lied so her mother wouldn't be mad at her for having sex.

Lucky for Norm, the Morality and Break & Enter units were combined in a department re-structuring. The Pawn Shop unit was also brought into the mix. The new group was called Street Crimes. The days off rotated, meaning officers worked with different partners all the time. One day he'd be investigating a B & E and the next he'd be locking up someone under the mental health act. There was no consistency and that drove him crazy.

There was one guy in the office that looked after all the pawn and second-hand shops in the city. City bylaws required the licensed second-hand stores to obtain identification from customers who were selling their goods. They also had to submit the paperwork to the police so they could check to see if the property was stolen. It was a daunting task.

There were hundreds of items sold every day and each serial number had to be checked manually against lists of stolen property. It's no wonder the old guy doing the job went off on a long-term sick leave. Stacks of paperwork piled up on the poor bastard's desk and nobody did his job while he was gone.

Norm worked on a B & E investigation that led him to a pawn shop to recover some stolen property. The rightful property owner had discovered their stolen jewelry at a local pawn shop. The investigation gave Norm a better insight to the pawn shop business. It also gave him an idea.

His boss had an office meeting one day and he said that he was looking for someone to take over the pawn job. Everyone looked over at the thousands of sheets of paper piled all over the corner desk, nobody wanted the job. Norm thought about the offer that night then went to see his boss the next morning. He told his boss he'd take on the job, but there were some conditions attached.

He told his boss he would only take the job if he could do it his way and that meant starting from scratch. There was no possible way to catch up on the months of paperwork that had piled up, so it had to be stuffed into boxes and filed away.

Norm also wanted to modernize the job with a better computer system, one that would search records automatically, look for stolen property, then pass on any hits to him. To sweeten the pot, he asked his boss to let him work different hours so he could overlap the pawn shops' operating hours and the office afternoon shift. It was better for communication and for the flow of information. He also hated getting up early.

Norm thought the idea of having his own desk and his own specific job would be cool and that nobody would bother him with all the other shit going on in the office. The boss was sold on his ideas of course, they would make him look good.

A part of the deal was to let him use two of the co-op students that were assigned to the office, they really hadn't been doing anything useful anyway. He put the two kids to work and had them haul all the paperwork down to the vault. The files had to be kept in the case that they were ever needed as evidence. While the kids were busy, Norm met with the computer programmer and the woman in charge of data entry.

While the computer geeks worked on his plan, he went out to introduce himself to all the pawn shop owners. He told them of the new automated system coming into effect and how they'd have to do their due diligence in completing the paperwork properly. Some owners hadn't given a shit previously and no one did anything about it.

Norm's research showed that 50 % of all property going through the pawn shops was stolen and the police didn't recover even one percent of it. Some of the shop owners weren't happy, but they knew it was better to cooperate with the police than to have them snooping around their store every day.

All pawn and second-hand shops had to be licensed by the city. A requirement of that license was that they had to request ID from all their customers, record all purchases including serial numbers, and then deliver the completed forms to the police. Norm then skimmed through the forms daily, selecting items that had the possibility of being stolen.

The students then entered those items into the city police computer system which automatically interfaced with a national data base for stolen property. Any hits on stolen property were then be sent back to Norm. The system worked. One or two hits a week started to roll in, Norm kept busy visiting the pawn shops and seizing stolen property from their shelves. The sellers were arrested and some victims actually got their stolen property returned to them.

Spinning

Norm's new pawn system pretty well ran itself as long as an investigator kept up to the daily paperwork and the students kept up with their data entry. He found out the hard way he needed someone to replace him and the students when they weren't around.

Although the boss had promised he'd have someone look after things, Norm returned from a vacation to find his desk buried almost as half as deep as when he took on the job. Nobody did a damn thing while he was gone. That was unacceptable. He trained another investigator to fill in for him and had the data entry clerks take up the slack between the groups of co-op students.

Co-operation between Norm and the B & E Squad led to the targeting of a group of *B & E boys* who were terrorizing the city. A provincial police investigator who visited regularly came into the office, compared notes and agreed that some of the same dirt bags were wreaking havoc in his jurisdiction.

A joint force operation *(J.F.O.)* was put together to combat the problem. Because of his past surveillance experience in the

Drug Squad, his knowledge of the B & E boys and perhaps as a bit of a reward, his boss assigned Norm to the J.F.O.

He was teamed up with the provincial investigator and their mobile surveillance *(Spin)* team. The city spin team was also phased in and used on occasion to follow specific targets that were known to be doing B & Es across the county. This meant Norm got his own car which would become his office for two months, while he worked with the J.F.O.

Mobile surveillance was always fun, it was the static surveillance that was a killer. There was nothing worse than getting stuck in the back of a freezing cold van in the middle of winter, having to piss in an empty juice bottle. As Norm had learned in the Drug Squad, spin teams used a whole different language to communicate over the radio.

With the provincial spin team, it was a different language but with many similarities. Not getting *burned* was the whole objective of a good spin. That means using at least five cars, so that different surveillance techniques can be used while watching specific targets. The goal was to catch them in the act of committing a crime.

On one occasion while being the *eye* Norm saw the target leave his residence on a bicycle. He lived outside the city. This guy was an experienced thief who did heat checks before heading out to do a B & E. Norm was parked about a half a block from the target's house on a side street.

The target rode out of his driveway and went about a half a block in the opposite direction. Then he circled back, riding past his house towards the street that Norm was parked on. He looked in Norm's direction, rode a short distance down that block and then turned around again.

Sure enough, he turned on the side street riding towards Norm. This target knew his neighborhood, a man sitting alone in a car parked around the corner from his house would not look right, he could easily assume that it was a cop. Without hesitation, Norm threw his coat over the mobile police radio that was in the back seat, then grabbed his clipboard and bailed out of the car.

There was a new house under construction across the street, so he walked up the driveway, and grabbed a hard hat off the back of a pick-up truck. He walked up to some guys working in a trench beside the house and pretended to be taking notes on the clipboard. The workers glanced up at Norm but continued their work.

The target stopped right beside Norm's car and looked in the window. He looked all around inside the car, then gazed over in Norm's direction. He started talking to the workers about a baseball game that had been on T.V. the previous night. The target got off his bike and stared at him and the workers for what seemed like an eternity. It was a good thing he had actually watched the game and had something to talk about.

The ruse worked and the target rode off into the neighboring town. Following a bicycle without being compromised turned out to be too much of a challenge for the spin team. This target was good, He purposely rode around the block, doing heat checks to see if anyone was following him. At one point, he placed his bike up against a tree and walked in between some houses.

Unfortunately for the police, you have to physically catch someone committing a crime before you can arrest them. In this case, that meant seeing the target break into a house, letting him steal something, and then arresting him with the goods on the way out. That was much easier said than done.

The spin team tried to surround the neighborhood and box the target in, but he came back out from between the houses and rode back to the commercial district. The team leader said he had the eye, and that the target went into a variety store.

Norm had some doubts about the skill level of the team leader and one other cop. They continually drove back and forth past the store instead of pulling in and parking somewhere. Even with his doubts, Norm was still shocked when the target came out of the store with a disposable camera and snapped pictures of the two spin team guys as they whizzed by trying not to look conspicuous. The gig was up, the team was officially burned.

Pawn Stars

Norm kept the Pawn Unit running smoothly and even had the city beef up some of its bylaws to put tighter restrictions on the stores. The opening of the casino brought a half dozen new pawn shops with it, some of which had shady reputations for practices like knowingly buying stolen property.

With information from one of his rats, Norm was able to obtain a search warrant to recover some unregistered stolen property from one downtown pawn shop. The owner had not been reporting his purchases of stolen property and fudging the serial numbers on property that he was reporting. The licensing committee felt sorry for the guy and only gave him a thirty-day suspension.

Reactive policing has been the norm since the inception of crime fighting. That was frustrating for Norm. He firmly believed in proactive policing…stopping crime before it actually happened. His rats played a huge part in that pursuit. A seminar on property crime was held up in Ottawa and Norm was ordered to attend.

There were a lot of great ideas kicked around at the conference. He made some good contacts and came away with a couple of ideas. One idea was to further computerize the local pawn industry, linking individual store computers with a national police system. The cost would have been mostly covered by the store owners. He presented the idea at a meeting with them and that's as far as it got.

The other idea was a pawn sting operation in which the police open their own pawn shop. It had been done successfully in another city. Norm thought it was a great idea since the thieves would be bringing their stolen property directly to the police. Police always had difficulty in obtaining information on whoever was fencing stolen property or where it all went.

Norm's buddy in the provincial police was also interested in the pawn shop idea, so Norm put together an operational plan and proposed a J.F.O. between the city and provincial police. He knew that bringing in manpower, and more importantly money from the provincial police, would make the project easier to sell locally.

Norm's boss was an easy sell, but he had to convince Ash Kist who was now the Deputy Chief. Kist was more concerned about the possible overtime hours, so Norm had to make promises that he wouldn't blow the overtime budget. Hence, *Project Copshop* was born.

Norm knew what it took to run a pawn shop, and he scoped out a few prime locations in the city. The provincial police brought in a few cops from out of town to help run the shop. They had to be cops who wouldn't be recognized in the city.

A location right in the heart of Motor Town was picked for the store. The rent was dirt cheap and there were plenty of criminals in the hood. An apartment on the outskirts of the city was rented as a safe house, the undercover cops *(U.C.'s)* needed a place to stay at night. The two U.C.'s both had fake ID with the first name of Joe, so the new store was called *Just Joe's*.

What the provincial police promised and what they actually delivered was far from the same, but Project Copshop got off the ground and opened for business. The two U.C.'s were not happy about being assigned to the project. It was a decision made after their former boss was transferred. Norm learned that he was getting their *has-beens*, but they would have to do.

The lead provincial investigator that was supposed to be his partner was re-assigned to other duties. The cop that replaced him was soon dragged into the daily store operation because the two Joe's were in over their heads, they were clueless about setting up and maintaining a store. Norm couldn't help with the store because he might be recognized in the hood, therefore compromising the whole project.

The cop crew managed to work out the kinks and the neighborhood punks started poking their noses into the store. The business was barely operational when the guy from the phone company installing the business phone offered to sell the store a bunch of stolen phones.

Norm visited the police property room in order to fill the store shelves with recovered property that was to be sold at auction. Getting the store set up and cutting through all the red tape was a difficult task, but not as difficult as keeping the whole project a secret. Cops are nosy by nature and his co-workers wanted to know what Norm was up to. He spent his time working from a laptop in the safe house, rather than in the office, just to avoid questions.

One of the local B & E boys went into the store one day and sold the guys a set of golf clubs, there was no doubt that he'd never even set foot on a golf course. The cops tried to get the thieves to admit the stuff was stolen. They said they wanted to know, so they could keep it *off the books* so the cops wouldn't know.

The transactions and conversations were all recorded on a surveillance camera. Others started to bring in their jewelry and what ever else they thought they could get a buck for. The U.C.'s started hanging out in the local bars, drumming up business, and getting known in the hood.

A hardcore, well-known criminal went into the store one day and asked the guys if they were interested in buying one hundred brand new car radios. The guy worked at Ford Motor Company and had been stealing them off the line, one at a time, for months. He said he'd sell the whole lot for four thousand bucks. One of the Joe's said he'd have to see a sample. The dirt bag complied and the cops were able to get the model and serial numbers.

Norm had to scramble, but was able to hook up with the head of Ford's security to see if the radios were missing. In the mean time, security said they'd cover the cost of buying the radios, so the deal was set up. Joe 1 went to the bank to get cash from the project *buy account*. Norm was horrified when he returned and showed him four one thousand-dollar bills.

"Who the hell would use such large bills for any kind of street deal?"

It was too late to exchange the money, the time and place for the deal had been set. Joe 1 said he needed a few minutes to get his police stuff out of the undercover pick-up truck.

"What the hell is the matter with you?" Norm asked out loud.

He learned that Joe 1 had been sneaking out of town at night with the company truck, going home to see his family. He even attended one of his kid's soccer games. He obviously didn't understand his priorities while working *undercover.* The deal was made and Joe 1 bought all the stolen radios.

The dirt bag asked Joe, "What the fuck am I supposed to do with these?" when he handed him the four crisp one thousand-dollar bills.

Bikers and Politics

Just Joe's was accepted as a normal business in Motor Town and the U.C.'s were accepted by the locals at the neighborhood bars. Joe 2 did an about face and really got into his role, he walked and talked the biker part. He even got invited to the local biker clubhouse. He was ecstatic. It was one of his life long goals as a U.C., to be able to infiltrate a biker gang. Norm had lost his patience with Joe 1, so the news from Joe 2 was a welcome reprieve.

The six-month project was almost at the half way point and the time had come for an evaluation from the brass. During the inception of the project, changes had taken place within the upper echelon of both police forces. A new chief was hired in the city and the provincial police shuffled around some of their brass who were overseeing Project Copshop.

The project team told the brass how they were just starting to see some good results and how Joe 2 had been invited into the local biker clubhouse.

It was the same clubhouse where their president had been murdered a few years earlier. A heated discussion ensued while the team defended the project and tried to explain how the biker infiltration could lead to great new possibilities. The brass balked, citing officer safety concerns. Joe 2 fumed, he was willing to take the risk. His superiors were not.

Norm couldn't offer up many criminal charges for the stolen property bought up to that point, it was difficult to prove that many of the items were actually stolen. According to the Crown Prosecutor, they would have had to rely on recent case law from similar situations to make their case. Manpower and money are always major issues within police budgets and that meant the end of Project Copshop.

Once again Norm had his project shut down before its time. Joe 1 was happy to go back home. Joe 2 was pissed off that he missed out on a good opportunity, but he had no choice in the matter.

New businesses came and went in Motor Town, so it was not unusual to see a store go out of business. The prosecutor wasn't sure about the reasonable expectation of securing convictions in the handful of cases the project spawned, so it was decided to keep the integrity of the project intact. No one was arrested or charged. The store was closed up and the remaining property was returned to the property room to be auctioned.

All the cops involved in the project were sent back to the units they originally came from. Norm was not a happy camper, once again the political powers to be had put the kibosh on one of his projects. He went back to his old pawn job in Street Crimes. It was business as usual for the bikers and criminals in Motor Town.

13
Mattress Mary

Mattress Mary could have been a nurse. She could have been a loving wife and mother of three children. She could have been a successful clothes designer. Instead, at an early age, Mary was chosen to be the victim of child abuse. Her mother's boyfriend taught her all about sex at the ripe age of ten.

Her mother didn't believe her accusations, so Mary became a runaway by the age of thirteen. She was book smart, but she soon traded in her books for street smarts. She was a pretty blonde girl with blue eyes and a nice figure. She could have easily been the high school prom queen. Instead of an academic high school, she went to the school of hard knocks.

Mary learned that she could put what her abuser had taught her to good use to get the things she wanted in life. The problem was that she hated her life, so she turned to drugs to make her feel better. The problem with her drug addiction was that she needed to find money to buy the drugs. Mary knew how to manipulate the system and she received government assistance. The money was never enough to feed her addiction, so she took to working the street, trading her body and self esteem for drugs.

The Italian Stallion

One of Norm's sergeants in the Drug Squad was known as the Italian Stallion. Someone gave him the nickname after seeing him in the showers, he was hung like a wild stallion. The Stallion liked to brag how about many bow-legged women were out there because of him. He was a legend in his own mind. There was one other thing that the Stallion was known for in the Drug Squad, he had a lot of informants. The strange thing was that most of them were females. The running joke in the office was that he *had* to be banging them.

The Stallion got a lot of calls from a rat he called M.M. The tips were usually related to crack dealers. Her tips were always good and the Drug Squad busted a lot of crack dealers on M.M.'s information. Like the majority of rats, M.M. was loyal to her handler and she only dealt with the Stallion.

Norm stumbled across some photos on the Stallion's desk one day and figured out that M.M. was in fact Mattress Mary. The Stallion kept pictures of Mary before and after her crack addiction. The two women in the pictures didn't even look related.

One night the Stallion said to Norm, "Let's go Storm, we gotta go meet M.M." They drove into the downtown projects where the Stallion pulled into an alley, then Mary jumped into the van.

She looked at Norm and said, "Hey big fella, you gotta smoke for me?"

The Stallion pulled a cigarette out of a pack he kept just for Mary. He introduced her to Norm. Mary reached over Stallion's shoulder and grabbed the whole pack before Stallion could put them away.

He just shook his head and said, "What have you got for me?"

"Fat Fiona's got a little nigger named "T" running for her. I'm gonna hook up with him."

Without missing a beat, Mary looked at Norm and said, "I hate niggers. You couldn't pay me enough to suck a nigger cock."

Norm choked; it must have been the cigarette smoke. Mary went on to tell the Stallion that she ordered up through Fat Fiona, who in turn sent T to meet Mary with the rock.

She looked at the Stallion, "You got fifty bucks so I can buy a rock?"

He and Mary bickered back and forth like an old married couple. He lectured her that he wasn't supporting her drug habit. Mary took a long drag on her cigarette and blew the smoke in his face.

"Okay, let me off up the road so I can find a John and make some money."

The Stallion wheeled around the corner. The van was barely stopped when Mary jumped out.

"I'll call ya later" she said, as she hopped out and ran across the street.

The Stallion just shook his head and asked Norm, "Are you hungry? Let's get something to eat."

The Stallion was always on some kind of fad diet. He took Norm to his favorite Chinese restaurant. He wasn't even half way through his house special-fried rice when his pager started vibrating.

He looked at the display and shook his head again, "Guess who? Shit, that was a quick trick."

The Stallion and Norm wolfed down their food, and then went to meet Mary again.

She jumped back in the van and said, "Okay, I got money, I need to get high."

"There's no way you did a trick that fast?"

"He was a two-minute wonder."

He told Mary she had cock breath. She leaned forward and blew on the side of his face trying to gross him out.

"Fuck-off Mary, where's the crack bastard now?"

Something's burning

The call was made, and Mary hooked up with T. The Stallion and Norm got a good look at him and the car he was driving. Mary ran back to the van and told the Stallion to drop her off down the road. Norm then heard the click of Mary's lighter and thought she was lighting up another smoke. He caught a weird smell in the air, like burning Styrofoam.

He looked back and saw Mary sucking on her crack pipe. She was smoking her rock right there in the van with him and the Stallion. Norm looked over at the Stallion. As usual, he just shook his head again and drove on.

T was busted later that night with a pocket full of crack. The Drug Squad knew he was running for Fat Fiona, but they couldn't prove it. They would have to wait for another day to get Fiona. Mary disappeared into the night...getting high, doing tricks and getting high. For her, it was the circle of life. She was a crack whore.

High & Dry

Norm got a call at work from the Italian Stallion one night. He was at home, but he told Norm that Mary was holed up in a flea bag motel. She was on the wagon and drying herself out. He was concerned about Mary since she had been on a five-day bender. That meant no eating or sleeping...just sucking on the pipe *(in more ways than one)*. He asked Norm if he could check in on her at the motel. Norm was only doing paperwork, so it was no big deal. It was more than a bit weird, going to a motel to check up on a crack whore.

Granted she was a prostitute and drug addict but in reality, she was a suffering human being, someone cops are sworn to protect.

Norm called the motel first to see if Mary was still there. The front desk put him through to her room. Mary answered the phone and he asked how she was doing.

She replied, "Oh, hey Storm. I'm okay, but I could really use a cup of tea."

Her voice was raspy, but quiet at the same time. She sounded like a little girl. She was usually loud and bouncing around like the energizer bunny. Crack does that to you. Norm told Mary he'd pop by with a tea.

She said, "You're such a sweetie. Can you bring me a pack of smokes too?"

That was the Mary he knew. She tried to get whatever she could take, and take whatever she could get. Norm drove out to the motel, stopping first to grab some smokes and a cup of tea. Mary was tucked into bed when Norm walked into the room. She got up to fix her tea and to light up a smoke. Norm chuckled at the Donald Duck flannel jammies Mary was wearing. She looked like a zombie from Night of the Living Dead goes to Disneyland.

Mary said, "Thanks for the tea, sweetie."

Norm and Mary fell into a conversation about nothing that turned into some sort of confession on her part. She spoke softly and told Norm how sick she was. Not just from the crack binge, but how her body was starting to shut down from all the different ailments she had. She listed the first part of the alphabet with the different hepatitis strains she had, along with her kidney and liver problems.

As Mary talked, Norm couldn't help but wonder what kind of men would actually pay this poor broken down woman for sex. He had heard from Mary and Squeaky Sally, how some men wanted to ride them bareback even after they were warned about the possibility of being infected with whatever diseases they had. According to the women, some men really are that stupid. Mary juggled her tea, her smoke, and the T.V. remote from hand to hand as she told Norm about her shitty life.

She didn't go into detail about what her stepfather did to her and her sister. Mary never talked about her sister; she didn't see her much. She mentioned her last failed relationship. Norm remembered Mary's lesbian lover Michelle, the guys in the office would joke and call it the Mike and Dyke show. They were always feuding, Mary would take off on a crack binge and Michelle would call the Stallion, giving up Mary's crack connections in hopes of finding her and getting her back home.

Norm listened like a big brother while she babbled on. She slowly crept deeper and deeper under the covers as she spoke.

She looked up at Norm said, "Thanks for coming by sweetie, I gotta crash now."

Mary reached up to give Norm a hug. He bent over the bed and she steered her lips towards Norm's. He politely turned a cheek and gave her a hug. It was sad to say, but Norm couldn't stop thinking about of all the diseases she carried.

Something about Mary

Mary was a crack head and she made no bones about how much she hated black men. The ironic part of that is that all of the crack dealers in the city at that time were black. At least that's the way it started when crack was introduced to the city. It was like the gold rush days of yesteryear, young black Americans flocked across the border looking to get rich. One lawyer accused Norm of being prejudice, that he was racially profiling his young black client.

The courtroom fell silent when Norm answered the question and said, "Yes."

Before the lawyer could regain his composure, Norm explained to the court how every crack dealer that he had arrested was black. Most of them were American. It was the simple truth.

Mary never really made any money being a rat. She mostly traded the information for a quick fix. Sometimes she'd have a prostitution charge to work off and she'd call the Drug Squad when the Stallion wasn't working or he was ignoring her calls. She'd give her information to whoever answered the phone in the hopes that she could trade up for a rock somewhere.

When the Stallion transferred out of the squad, Mary worked with the other cops in the unit, becoming a squad rat. It was always all about Mary. Like any crack head, she said, or did anything to score her next high.

When Norm transferred out of the Drug Squad to the Morality unit, it was Mary who he found sexually engaged in the alley that night.

There was another time when he was doing surveillance in Motor Town, watching the undercover pawn shop. Mary came up from behind him, opened the passenger door, and jumped in the front seat.

Before he realized who she was, Mary said, "Hey Storm, you got a smoke?"

That was Mary. Every time Norm saw her, it shocked and saddened him to see how much that she had deteriorated physically.

The last time he saw Mary was a couple years before he retired, while he was investigating an arson in Motor Town. She looked like a sixty-year-old woman. She was all skin and bones and her once pretty face was hollowed and sunken in.

Mary was dying a slow and miserable death. She looked over at Norm from the sidewalk and offered up a half of a smile. Norm nodded in response as Mary walked away down the sidewalk. He watched her as she disappeared around the corner and he wondered, what would become of Mary?

Life can be cruel. Mary is a living example of it.

14
Politics and Promotion

"Nearly all men can stand adversity, but if you want to test a man's character, give him power."
– Abraham Lincoln

It took 20 years, but Norm Strom was finally promoted to the rank of sergeant. It took him longer than most, but he earned the promotion all on his own, he owed no one. He refused to cheat on the promotional exams like some of his co-workers and felt that promotions should be the reward for good work.

Unfortunately, that wasn't the case with the promotional system that was in place. Norm had no aspirations of climbing the company ladder, but a promotion meant more money and more job opportunities.

He had made the decision a few months prior to his promotion to lose some serious weight and to get his ass back into shape. The process took almost a year, but Norm lost a shit load of weight through proper diet and exercise. That meant no more fast food, beer, or wine.

The first order of business upon his being promoted was to be welcomed to the management team by the Chief of police. As Norm's luck would have it, Ash Kist had risen through the ranks to the Chief's position. Kist was the man who said Norm would never get a plain clothes job if he had anything to do with it. Six years later, after working in plain clothes doing investigations, he was now a member of Kist's management team.

It was a routine welcome aboard speech given by the Chief in his office. He told Norm what was expected of him as a supervisor and leader in the organization. He congratulated him on the promotion and asked him if he had any questions.

Norm couldn't resist, he just had to ask, "Yes Chief, now that I'm part of your team, I was just wondering what exactly it is that you don't like about me?"

The chief had obviously gotten better at playing poker over the years, he didn't turn red like the last time Norm asked.

"I have no problem with you at all Norm."

"I've been curious all these years chief, I'd like to know if it is something that can be fixed."

"I don't know what you're talking about."

It was important for Norm to know his allies and his enemies, but the chief wouldn't reveal his hand. The match was a draw, but he had no doubt the chief was holding a couple of aces.

The New Centurions

Getting promoted to sergeant meant that Norm had to get a hair cut and put a uniform back on. He was told by the big boss that he had to take his turn back in the monkey suit like everyone else. Well, not really everyone else, a few of Kist's golden boys managed to stay in plain clothes, being promoted to detective instead of sergeant *(they are the same rank)*. His hard work in drugs and B & E didn't make any difference to the brass, he was just another body to fill a position.

Norm had always promised himself that if he ever got to be a sergeant, he would lead by example and try to pass on any valuable lessons that he had learned from his past experiences. The majority of the patrol officers that he was commanding were much younger and had no investigative experience.

He wrote out a whole list of things and planned to give his platoon a tip each and every day before they hit the streets. He hoped that by sharing his expertise he could help them to become better street cops. So, each day at roll call Norm offered a *tip of the day* after reading out the assignments and bulletins.

He noticed right from the start that something had changed since his uniform days. There was no more camaraderie among the platoon. Each man and woman seemed to be out for themselves, it was a new breed for sure. He asked them what kind of socializing they did as a platoon.

One of the guys said, "We don't do anything together."

"What, you guys don't go out for beers together?"

"Nope, we've never done that."

Norm firmly believed that he needed to sit down and share a few cocktails with someone in order to really get to know them and eventually trust them. Getting someone out of their working environment and loosening them up with a couple drinks, was a sure way to let their true personalities show through.

His first order of business was to coordinate a night out for the entire platoon. There were some cops who didn't talk to others and some that said they didn't drink or see the need to go out. Norm really didn't care if they drank or not, they were all going to go out as a group.

The only way to get everyone out for the night was to do it when they were all at work *(the platoons were set up in such a way that everyone had the same days off)*. He arranged for one of the other platoons to cover for his at the end of an afternoon shift. That meant that everyone would have to put in a chit for two hours off.

Some of the platoon was not happy about taking time off to go out with their co-workers, so Norm spelled out the rules to them. Everyone had to put in a chit and everyone would attend. For those who thought they'd just take the time off and go home, he told them he would process their chit. For anyone who went out with the group he said he'd hold on to their chits for a while, eventually letting them disappear. It was basically a bribe, giving them free company time to go out together as a group.

His plan worked. Everyone showed up, even a couple of the guys who never socialized with anyone. Some beers and wings and a lot of laughs were had. One of the guys even asked Norm what the tip of the day was going to be the next day. Another said what a great idea it was getting together and going out. The smiles on their faces and the jocular mood proved to Norm it was the right thing to do.

He had managed to bring the platoon a little closer together, letting them know who the people backing them up really were. In police work their lives sometimes depended on each other. The camaraderie some how found its way back to his platoon. They came to work with a smile on their faces and most of them seemed eager to learn something new each day.

Leading by example was part of Norm's game plan, but he soon found out that things had changed out on the street. The patrol cars were all computer dispatched, leaving minimal chatter over the radio. He had to search the computer to find out where his people were. In the old days, you knew what everyone was up to by listening to the radio.

With the new system, no one knew what anyone else was doing. The system isolated everyone out on the street. In his opinion, it was dangerous when no one else knew what you were up to. It was also boring just watching calls pop up on a computer screen and not being able to hear all the action going on.

There was also a new breed of cop on the street, they were being hired older and with families. Men and women in their thirties or forties were trying to do a job that Norm had found difficult at twenty. Their minds were on their families at home and not on the job at hand. Cell phones were becoming popular, one guy shocked Norm when his phone rang out loud and he answered it while on a service call.

Some were afraid to get involved, for the fear that they might end up getting their asses sued. The old street wise cops were gone, replaced by report takers. Calls for service were endless, his platoon went from call, to call, to call. There was no down time for writing tickets or for hunting down bad guys.

Going Back

Norm worked as a patrol sergeant for about six months, then he jumped at the opportunity to get back into plain clothes. He applied for a detective spot on the B & E Squad in the Street Crimes office. He came out of the interview with a good feeling. His old Street Crimes boss was on the interview panel and told him he was a shoe in.

The next day, one of the golden boy's names appeared on the transfer order. The boss just shook his head and told Norm that he had the job when he left the room. The decision had been made higher up. As fate would have it, the golden boy got himself in trouble several years later, he was caught on video beating an innocent man and he lost his job.

Another plain clothes posting came up, this time for an opening in the Drug Squad. Norm's buddy Jesse James was being transferred out, so he and Norm switched jobs. Norm went back in Drugs, this time as a sergeant and once again working for Teflon Tim.

He knew most of the cops who'd be working for him, and he had worked along side a few of them in the past. The other sergeant in the squad was Norm's old Drug Squad buddy Blackjack. He and Norm now had to supervise the cowboys, instead of being one of them. Blackjack gave Norm the heads up right away as to who the troublemakers were. He had already butted heads with a few of them. He wished Norm luck and welcomed him back into the squad.

New Sherriff in Town

Teflon Tim also welcomed Norm back. He said there was a new breed in the Drug Squad too, they had to be hand-fed their work with a silver spoon. Go figure, they were glorified secretaries on patrol and they never had the time or the desire to investigate anything. The Drug Squad was supposed to be a training ground for investigators, but the new breed thought they knew it all coming in.

Tim told Norm that the unit was splintered into three separate groups, each one hating the other. He asked him to look into that and see what he could do. He also asked Norm to give him progress reports on any changes that might come about.

Most people can be supervised, but it's much easier to supervise a person than their ego. There were a few too many big egos in the Drug Squad. All the search warrants, seizures, arrests and projects that Blackjack and Norm had under their belts meant nothing to the new breed.

They took short cuts in any way that they could and always looked for the easy way out. A few of the lazy ones actually used a template for their search warrants, they just changed the names and addresses in the information to obtain the warrant.

Not all lawyers are completely stupid, Norm warned them what would happen if they got caught. None of the unit cared about their investigative files, they only wanted the easy busts.

Blackjack told him he had some of the same concerns, but his help was unwanted and his suggestions had been ignored.

As asked by his boss Tim, Norm kept him in the loop by leaving tape recorded phone messages letting him know what was going on during the night shifts. The unit started to rebel against Blackjack and Norm. They acted like children and turned to playing games like paging their sergeants with each other's phone numbers or the *gay* hotline. They even sent a pizza to Blackjack's house one night.

After some time, Norm helped bring the unit closer together as a whole, but he some how alienated himself at the same time. This all should have been no surprise to him who had gone through some of the same crap, back when he had sergeants over him in the unit.

The Italian Stallion had told Norm once, "What goes around comes around." He was so right.

Passing the Torch

Some new blood was introduced into the unit in the form of transfers and things got a bit better. Norm still had a few active informants and relied on them to drum up some action for the unit. To get their feet wet, Norm signed off on a couple of his informants, letting the new investigators work with them.

He saw potential in one guy and gave him some of his old files on Michael Cook, so he could learn how to do some digging. A younger Drug Squad cop had tried to take down Cook after Norm left the unit. He had warned him that the money and drugs would never be in the same place at the same time, but he tried anyway. Cook was nowhere near the thirty-five grand that was recovered. No drugs were found and the money had to be returned.

One of the provincial police sergeants tried to get a J.F.O. going with Cook as one of the targets, but he couldn't put an attractive enough package together to convince the brass to run the project. About a year later, the R.C.M.P. took a run at the same group who were deeply connected to the outlaw bikers in the area.

Norm took his protégé along to the meeting and he ended up being seconded to the J.F.O. They later took down some of the bikers and put a dent in their cocaine business, but Cook remained unscathed. He had moved out of the city and had taken on a larger role within the criminal enterprise.

Some of the new blood did well in the Drug Squad, but there was still a small group that had something against Norm and he could never figure out exactly what it was. Even more frustrating was the fact that one of those guys had been partners with Norm in uniform.

It wasn't until about a year later after Norm transferred out of the Drug Squad that he found out what the problem was. Jesse had transferred back into the unit again and one of the guys told him that Norm was a rat. Teflon Tim had called the guys into his office one morning, played his phone messages and said, "Here, listen to what your sergeant has to say about you."

Tim sold out Norm, trying to win favor with the guys even though he had asked him to try and fix things. That explained why he got the cold shoulder from the unit. He had bent over backwards for them and even looked the other way a few times when they broke the law, while trying to enforce the law.

Norm took the next opening in the B & E Squad, and he transferred back into Street Crimes as a sergeant/detective. It was once again a supervisory role, but he was expected to conduct and lead property crime related investigations. The Street Crimes branch consisted of the B & E, Morality, Auto

Theft, and the Pawn Shop units. Norm was right at home since he had worked in most of those areas before. His boss was transferred out and Norm's old training officer Andy Green was put in charge.

Norm's connections on the street were of great help in solving some break-ins and recovering some stolen cars. He had also worked with the Morality sergeant in the past so the two men were able to work in harmony when Norm's hooker informants wanted to trade information for the withdrawal of their charges.

Street Crimes was a good home for Norm, he liked the shifts and the fact he got to wear jeans to work again.

15
Louie the Wop

L ouigi Finghetti was probably born and raised as an upstanding Catholic boy who went to church every Sunday and did his time as an alter boy. Somewhere along the way, he fell off the path of God. His quest was to see how many of the commandments he could break. Norm knew Louie was a con man the moment that he met him. He pretended he was a do-gooder when he called Norm, saying that he wanted to get his girlfriend back on the path of righteousness.

With several years of experience in handling informants, Norm knew better. It was protocol to check police records for any new prospective informant. Louie had a bit of a criminal record, with one conviction for arson. He was hired to set someone's car on fire and burned himself in the process.

Louie liked to yap on the phone, but Norm insisted they meet so he could get a better feel for the anxious caller. He met up with Norm and climbed out of a beat up old pick-up truck with a wheel barrow and some shovels in the back. Along with the truck and its load, Louie had "typical Italian" written all over him. He had wavy black hair that was starting to recede back on his well-tanned forehead.

His two-day stubble beard probably looked sexy to some women, but Norm thought it just added to Louie's disheveled look. He wore a wife-beater shirt with torn jeans and work boots, and introduced himself as Louie the Wap. He said he was self-employed in the cement business, go figure.

Love is blind

Louie told Norm that his girlfriend was a coke head, and that he was afraid that her two small children were being exposed to a life that he didn't think was fair to them. It was obvious to him that Louie was infatuated with his girlfriend, as he described her and the fact that she had been a stripper when he met her. There it was...lonely guy in bar falls for stripper, how cliché.

Anyway, Louie seemed sincere in his concern for his drug abusing girlfriend and the welfare of her children. It was difficult for Norm to figure out exactly where Louie fit in since he said that he was actually living at his mom's but staying with his girlfriend.

Louie was another sucker in that long line of do-gooders, who thought he could stop his girlfriend from doing coke by having her dealers busted. It really didn't matter to Norm since his job was busting drug dealers. He was a sergeant in the Drug Squad when he met Louie. He had considered handing him off to one of his subordinates, but quite frankly, none of them were deserving of a free handout at the time.

Norm had the time, so he followed up on Louie's information and staked out his girlfriend's place whenever he said that she had placed an order for coke. It didn't take Norm long to figure out that Louie was partying right along with his girlfriend Patty. The more he called and talked to Norm, the more he was convinced of his earlier suspicions that Louie was a smooth-talking con artist.

He got the impression that Louie trusted Patty about as far as he could throw her; she was a stripper turned shooter girl after all, and somewhat of a con artist herself.

If anyone's ever been to a strip club, they'd have noticed that the shooter girls have more body contact than most of the strippers. They don't take the bit of clothes that they're wearing off, but they dance all over you and your lap while trying to feed you a watered-down shot with a fancy name like *sex on the beach*. Norm believed that Louie's real fear was that Patty was trading sex for coke when he wasn't around. He said she never had any money for the stuff, he was always lending her cash. Either way, Louie was intent on setting up Patty's coke dealers.

Some of the things Louie said led Norm to believe that he wanted the dealers busted so he didn't have to pay his debt to them. Dealers sometimes "front" their customers the dope until they have the cash to pay them. It's pretty hard for the dealers to collect money owed to them while they are in jail.

Louie called Norm frequently, but he could never seem to put himself and the coke dealers on the same page. In the meantime, he let the cat out of the bag in regards to other guys he knew who were dealing coke. They were his own buddies or dealers who had nothing to do with his girlfriend.

Some of the names Louie dropped easily caught Norm's attention, since they were well-known to the Drug Squad. The one guy was a high-level dealer with outlaw biker connections, and another was a part owner of a local business. Norm tried to steer Louie in their direction instead of constantly stalking his girlfriend's dealers.

Louie finally came through with a noon time phone call to Norm saying that Patty was taking delivery of two 8-balls, or a quarter of an ounce of coke. Time passed slowly and the information changed, as things often do in the drug world.

It wasn't until 8pm that Norm was able to put the grab on a guy who left Patty's house with an 8-ball of coke. He wasn't the original dealer, but he had the hot potato and got busted with it. It wasn't a total waste of time; Norm made some overtime cash and Louie got paid a fifty-dollar reward for his tip.

Money Motivated

A taste of money was all Louie needed to keep him calling. Within three weeks, he was on the horn again with Norm, this time ratting out the DJ at the bar where Patty worked. Louie said that the DJ was dealing coke to the staff and patrons in the bar, including Patty. Once Patty made a buy, Louie dropped a dime to Norm telling him that she scored and that the DJ was holding.

Norm pinched the DJ with twenty-three grams of coke individually packaged for sale, along with a bit of weed, two hundred and fifty bucks in cash and his pager. At that time, powder cocaine was selling on the street for a hundred dollars per gram. Louie had hoped to get Patty busted too, but her search came up clean. That tip earned Louie a C note.

There were three ways that informants could make money from the police. As mentioned in an earlier chapter, informants could be police agents and sign a contract to be paid money for their information and involvement. The drawback was that they would later have to testify in open court. The easiest way for an informant to make money was to anonymously call Crime Stoppers and give their information over the phone.

Crime Stoppers did not record the calls and issued the informants a personal identification number. The informants called back later using their ID number to see what, if any, police action was taken. If arrests or drug seizures were made, the informant was directed to a specific business location where they identified themselves by their ID number, then they were given an envelope containing their cash reward.

Louie the Wop was a registered city police informant. That meant that Norm had signed him up, and that his name went into a special vault that was only accessible by the officer in charge of the Intelligence Branch. After making an arrest and/or seizure, he had to submit a report to the officer in charge of the Investigation Division, requesting a cash reward for the informant. Whether it was Crime Stoppers or the police directly, the rewards were usually minimal.

Crime Stoppers was privately funded, so big busts could net informants up to a maximum of one thousand dollars. Norm only had one case where such a reward was paid out, the Drew Dancer bust. Police reward money came from unclaimed, found or seized property that had been auctioned off. It was difficult to get an informant any more than a couple of hundred bucks from that source, no matter how big the bust was.

Bigger Fish to Fry

Louie was on and off with Patty, but he relished the fact that he was still banging her; she had taken up with some bikers who were also banging her. It seemed that she would spread her legs for anyone with coke. Norm asked Louie if he was double bagging himself before he fucked Patty, but he just laughed in response. He supplied Norm with some information on the bikers and some other coke dealers the Drug Squad was interested in.

In the meantime, he gave up Patty and some other guy to Norm one night, he was probably pissed off that he hadn't banged her in a while. Norm was able to arrest them in the guy's car. They were both in possession of a small amount of cocaine.

The R.C.M.P. had an interest in a high-level supplier that Louie was connected to. Norm took one of his keener Drug

Squad guys to a meeting with the Mounties and shared the information that he had on the drug kingpin. Norm's keener became part of their J.F.O. He introduced him to Louie so that he could get information directly from the source. He would have loved to have been part of the J.F.O but Norm's rank meant that he wasn't eligible.

The project went almost a year, before the kingpin was taken down with a bunch of his cronies. The Mounties seized his house, boat, fancy cars and a motorcycle, along with a whack of cash, under the proceeds of crime act.

The Mounties let Norm continue to use Louie in an attempt to get a smaller player who was involved in their project. The theory being, that if Norm was able to get one of the smaller fish, he might lead them to the big fish. The mid-level dealer was partners with a guy whose family owned a local sporting goods store.

Louie told Norm that a lot of the deals were made after hours in the store in a party room upstairs. On one particular night, Louie told Norm there was a half a pound of coke coming to the store to be separated between the two partners. The Drug Squad set up surveillance and waited for all the players to get in place.

Murphy's Law applies to drug work; if something can go wrong, it will. Piecing together Louie's information and trying to identify the various targets in the dark proved to be difficult. Norm acted on the information he had and raided the store. Only the younger brother of the coke dealer was at the store and it seemed that he wasn't involved. The store was huge and the search came up empty.

As it turned out, one of the dealers had the exact same type of car that the brother had and the Drug Squad missed the bad guys leaving with some of the dope. Louie later told Norm that the brother who got away flushed three ounces of coke down the toilet when he thought the cops were coming for him.

Things didn't work out as planned that night and to make it worse, one of the drug cops left his notebook containing highly sensitive information, in the store. He wasn't able to retrieve it until the next day, it was not a good thing.

As fate would have it, the younger brother was arrested a few years later for several charges of attempted murder. He was H.I.V. positive and he had infected several city women. He knowingly infected the women, not caring about the consequences. The innocent looking little brother was the real bad ass in the family. It came out in the media later, that the mother knew about his condition, no one did anything to stop him. He was convicted and will be in jail for a very long time.

Project Pop Shop

Norm was itching for a good project to sink his teeth into and Louie helped to deliver the goods. He told Norm about a downtown variety store that was buying/selling/trading stolen property and drugs.

Louie said, "You can get a coca-cola and cocaine at the same store."

He also said that he heard that the brothers who ran the place were selling guns. When describing the store's location, Louie said one brother ran the massage parlor next door.

Louie chuckled and said, "Ya man, you can get high and get off there."

He said that the owner, or one of his girls sold you weed or coke, along with the massage. George liked getting massaged there because the girls offered him a *happy ending*. That's all Norm had to hear, it covered all the bases for a Street Crimes project…drugs, guns, and sex. He ran the idea of a project by his boss Andy Green. Andy liked it and ran it by his boss. He told Norm to write up an operation plan.

An operational plan can be simple or complex, depending on the type of investigation. It is like a flow chart in words, describing how you will go about conducting an investigation. It has to include the personnel and equipment to be used, as well as the target(s) and what exactly the criminal activity is that the project will focus on. It's a playbook for the brass so that they know exactly what the context of the investigation is and what the proposed outcome will be.

Since drugs and guns were really beyond the scope of the Street Crimes branch, Norm brought his buddy Jesse from the Drug Squad on board, along with someone from the Provincial Weapons Unit. Norm not only needed manpower from the other units, he needed buy money.

The mandate in Street Crimes covered any stolen property purchased, but not drugs or guns. The provincial unit had lots of money earmarked to take illegal guns off the street, so Norm took advantage of that. He also had to bring the Spin Team on board for surveillance on the targets and different locations involved.

With all the different units, manpower, and money in place there were only two things missing, a lead investigator and an undercover operator. Norm was a supervisor in Street Crimes, so he suggested one of his investigators, Mickey D, take on the roll of lead investigator. That meant he'd have to do all the grunt work while Norm supervised and oversaw the whole project.

Andy Green's boss didn't except Norm's suggestion for an out-of-town U.C. and he went with one of their own guys from the Drug Squad. Cheech had taken the U.C. course and had acquired a little drug experience, but it is always a risk doing undercover work in your own city. Norm agreed on the condition he would act as Cheech's handler. The handler is responsible for the U.C. and their actions.

Getting In

The most difficult part of an investigation for an undercover operator is getting next to, or being accepted by, the bad guys. They have to dress for and play a role, according to the situation at hand. In this case, the variety store was the main target, with the massage parlor next door as a secondary target. Two of the three brothers who ran the store were the main players; one of them ran the massage parlor and also dealt drugs from his house.

Cheech's job was to befriend these guys and eventually make some buys from them. You would think an introduction from Louie the Wop would be the way to go but then he'd have to testify in court later on. That would not be good for Louie.

Using the background information from Louie, Cheech took on the identity of a local street urchin who was looking to make a buck any way he could. To make the project operational, Norm had to have special briefings in advance with the bosses and then with everyone from Street Crimes, Drugs, and Surveillance who were involved. It was a dangerous gig for Cheech, officer safety is paramount.

He was given a special pager that was really a transmitter. The cover team was able to listen in on any of his conversations. Cheech would use a special code word in the case of an emergency and the cavalry would rush to his rescue. Norm requisitioned some gold bling and electronics from the property room. The bling was for show and Cheech was to attempt to sell the electronics as stolen property.

One Stop Shopping

On Cheech's first visit to the store, he scored an 8-ball of coke for two hundred bucks and two electronic calculators. He was in. He made arrangements with one of the brothers to come back later in the week and buy a quarter ounce of coke *(2 8-balls or 7grams)*.

On the second visit Cheech tried to unload a camcorder at the store. He bought a quarter ounce of coke and ten ecstasy pills for five hundred and twenty dollars. The goal for the rest of the project team was to see exactly where the stolen property and drugs were coming from and going to. The team had to follow the brothers and their friends back and forth from the store to various houses in the city.

On his third visit, he traded the camcorder and a hundred in cash for a laptop and an X Box. During his conversation with the one brother, Cheech was offered more ecstasy, cocaine, and guns. The project team made the decision to try and buy more cocaine and guns. They would attempt to see where the stuff was coming from at the same time.

Cheech returned to the store for the fourth time and bought a .32 caliber hand gun for four hundred and fifty dollars and an 8-ball of coke for two-twenty. He left a laptop at the store for a future trade. The target told him he could have sex next door at the massage parlor if he wanted. He also offered Cheech larger amounts of coke and more guns. Mickey D checked the gun Cheech bought and found that it had been reported stolen.

He went back to the store a fifth time and was able to buy an ounce of cocaine for fourteen hundred dollars. The project team made the decision there was enough evidence to search the store, massage parlor, and one house. There was also enough evidence to arrest two of the brothers for drug trafficking and possession of stolen property. The three search warrants were all executed at the same time on the same night.

Cheech had ordered up some more coke just prior, so the team would have the chance to get some more of the drug off the street. The cops found some weed and cash while searching the store, along with the electronics he had traded them. More cash and stolen property were seized from one brother's house.

Three women were arrested at the massage parlor and charged with various drug and prostitution charges. Two of the three brothers were charged with an assortment of criminal charges.

Mickey D almost pulled out what little hair he had left, trying to wrap up the project and complete the mountains of paperwork that went with it. Norm was in his element, loving the pressure and multi-tasking that went along with such a gig. He thrived in those work environments.

Norm didn't hear from Louie the Wop after Project Pop Shop. He got his reward and stayed in touch on and off with the younger Drug Squad guy that Norm had introduced him to. The last that Norm heard, Louie he was doing a stint in jail. His life was set, like the cement that he worked with. It would always be the same. He did whatever he could to make a buck.

16
Fraudsters

*"I hated every minute of my training, but I said, 'Don't quit.'
Suffer now and live the rest of your life as a champion."*
– Muhammad Ali

Just when Norm was enjoying a good run in Street Crimes, the powers to be decided that another of their golden boys needed some investigative experience, so they gave him Norm's job. His buddy Digger Daniels called him on the Labor Day holiday weekend to give him the good news. Norm was up north on his annual fishing trip with the boys when he got the call. His old car partner wanted to congratulate him personally on his transfer to the Fraud Squad.

It was the last place he wanted to go; he had even spelled that out on the fancy new skills inventory forms that everyone had to fill out months earlier. The form was basically an interdepartmental resume, where you listed your job experience and where you might like to work in the future. Norm checked the box specifying he did *not* want to go to Fraud.

The horrified look on Norm's face prompted one of the guys to hand him a beer and ask him what had happened. He had checked the box for the Arson job. Daniels tried to make him feel better by telling him that the Arson Unit worked out of the Fraud Squad. They filled the Arson job with another golden boy who had absolutely no investigative experience.

It made no sense at all, but the brass did that kind of thing to give certain people more experience before their next promotion. Fraud had been known as a dead-end position for mostly senior guys that nobody else wanted. Norm was in shock, so he took some extra vacation time before returning to work.

It had been a rough year for him personally, they say shit comes in threes, he had his triple whammy. He separated from his wife, his dad had a heart attack and his mom got cancer. The separation became a divorce. His dad recovered with a double bypass, but his mom died of the cancer. There was one point where he actually got to visit both parents on the same day in the same hospital.

Norm's strength came from the fact that each event distracted from the other. He was the eldest sibling and had to be strong for the others. Work was a distraction too; it kept his mind off his personal life.

The New Fraud Squad

He showed up for his first day in the Fraud Squad with his left arm in a sling. He had been out on his motorcycle and had a spill, fracturing his left elbow. It was strictly an office job, so he figured he might as well suffer on company time.

Once again, he had to trade in his jeans and break out the dress shirts and ties. There had been quite a few transfers while Norm was away, they did that every once in a while, to shake things up and to prevent stagnation in areas where some people worked forever.

Norm had worked with his new boss before; he was not happy with the transfers either. He said he was trying to give the Fraud Squad a new image and turn things around. That task seemed pretty well impossible since there was a two-year backlog of fraud files. That meant that Norm had thirty files stacked up in his computer queue, waiting to be addressed.

Norm had one thing going for him. His new boss had previously been the arson investigator and he was not happy about the new arson investigator who had no investigative experience. He knew Norm was interested in the job, so he asked him if he wanted to be the backup arson investigator *(it was normally a one-man job)*.

The boss hoped that Norm could offer the new guy some investigative support, an area where he had years of previous experience. It was an offer too good to refuse, he knew that by taking the offer that the arson job would be his in the future.

Fraud is complicated. It's probably one of the reasons that nobody wanted to work in that office. The files were long and involved, sometimes with hundreds of pages of documents to read over. The only saving grace was that the lengthy paper trail eventually led to the criminal who instigated it.

Norm was completely overwhelmed at first. He got to go to the police college for a two-week fraud course, which helped him get a better understanding of the crime. He also knew everyone in the office, having worked with them at some point during his career.

The workload was heavy, but for the most part everyone carried their own weight. Norm did what he always did, he dug in and did his job. It wasn't long before he got called in to assist the arson investigator, he needed a search warrant and had never written one. Norm had about a hundred and fifty search warrants under his belt, so he became the tutor.

Magic Plastic

While he tried to figure out just exactly what fraud was all about, the other guys in the office did show and tell with some of their investigations to bring him up to speed. One of the guys was just finishing up a huge counterfeit investigation where the fraudster had mastered counterfeiting various government documents and American Express travelers' checks.

Norm was amazed at the quality of the documents; he would have never detected the counterfeits on his own. Even more amazing was the fact that the head of security from American Express said that the counterfeit checks were the best that he'd ever seen.

The checks were in Canadian funds, that's how the dummy got caught. An alert sales person noticed the guy spelled *Canadian* wrong on the top of the checks. Prior to getting caught, he had cashed in about two hundred grand in phony checks. He traveled and bought all kinds of stuff, including two luxury vehicles.

Norm got called into his boss's office one day and saw his buddy Jesse sitting there with one of the other fraud guys. Jesse said that one of his informants got busted for a bunch of arrest warrants, and he was looking to trade information for a get out of jail free card.

Norm and his fellow fraud investigator were well aware of who this long- time criminal was, he had been a target on their joint wire tap when Norm was in Drugs and he was in the B & E Squad. The information he wanted to trade was all fraud related, so Jesse brought it to the Fraud Squad. Karl Crest was in the cell block waiting to be interviewed, so Norm's boss told him to do the interview with one of Jesse's drug investigators.

Norm thought he'd heard it all after twenty-five years on the job, but he was in for another lesson in crime. Karl Crest had been a thief most of his life. He told Norm he was stealing credit cards and selling them to a guy named "Roy" on the west side of the city.

Karl also had a girlfriend who was *skimming* credit cards at a local restaurant. Crest said she was given an 8-ball of coke a week for skimming the cards. The girl carried a mini credit card reader in her apron, where she swiped the customer's card through the device before swiping it again at the cash register.

This was all new to Norm, he was in awe. Karl said he took the loaded skimmer to Roy who then downloaded the credit card data onto his laptop in the back room of the store that was run by his buddy Nazim. Karl said that he had given Roy the data from at least fifty stolen credit cards.

The deal was that Karl had to supply information and work with Norm if he wanted to be released on bail. The assistant crown attorney was not impressed with the information alone, he wanted Karl to swear to a written statement before he would consider releasing him.

Even though Jesse vouched for Karl, Norm had been burned by informants before and he knew that if Karl got released, he'd probably never hear from him again. He had to milk Karl for all he was worth before letting him out of his sight. Norm grabbed Karl as soon as he was released from jail and took him for a ride.

On the way to Roy's place, Karl told Norm he had a guy working at major electronics store who'd let him use the stolen credit cards to buy plasma TV's and other electronics. Karl then sold the electronics on the street for up to fifty cents on the dollar. Norm drove Karl right to Nazim's store where Roy worked in the back.

The deal was that Karl was supposed to get Norm a sample card from Roy, but he was uncomfortable when Karl showed up. The word might have gotten out that Karl got busted, Roy said he didn't have any cards to give him.

Credit Card Skimming 101: Karl stole someone's wallet and credit cards. Roy took the cards and ran them through his skimmer, obtaining all the data or information that is encoded on the black stripe on the back of the card. Roy then took that information and transferred it to a new blank card, or one that he had previously wiped clean.

He had software that allowed him to ascertain the limit on the cards. Roy sold the cards to guys like Karl who went on shopping sprees buying merchandise. They sold the goods on the street for cash. The scary thing is that a guy like Karl could have a Visa card with his name on the front, but all the information on the back belonged to someone else. It is a very lucrative scam.

Norm had a lot to think about and even more follow-up to do on the people and addresses that Karl gave him. He spent the whole next day trying to absorb all the new information. Karl never checked in with him, that was no surprise.

Another day passed with no word from Karl but one of the drug cops called Norm with more information on Roy and "Nazim," the guy who ran the store. He now had enough information to prepare a search warrant for the store and Roy's apartment above it. The boss was impressed. With the exception of searches on bank records, the fraud guys had never used informants or did search warrants on houses.

Hip Deep

While Norm was busy prepping his search warrants, the office got a call from uniformed officers who had arrested two guys with a bunch of cloned debit cards and a whack of cash, all in twenty-dollar bills. They had been caught in the act at a local bank machine, using the cloned debit cards to withdraw cash from other people's bank accounts.

The cops caught the guys with seventeen blank debit cards and seven thousand dollars in cash. They had grounds to believe there was more evidence in their vehicle, so that meant getting a search warrant. Norm was volunteered to write the warrant.

The shit was piling up in the fraud office and Norm was in it hip deep. After all was said and done, seventy-one cloned cards and almost thirty thousand in stolen cash was recovered. The Fraud Squad got noticed, the brass was ecstatic. They even put on a show and tell news release for the media.

(The cloned debit cards worked the same way...stolen personal information was encoded on the magnetic strip on the cards, giving access to the bank accounts. PIN numbers had also been stolen and attached to the cards)

Norm had no time to bask in the glory, he had two more search warrants to finish in order bust Roy and Nazim at the variety store. He absorbed and learned as he went along, it was on the job training. The Fraud and Drug Squads raided the variety store, arresting Roy and Nazim.

The cops seized clone cards, stolen cards, two laptops, fake ID, credit card information, and debit machines. Norm later learned how the guys had put a special chip into the debit card machines to steal the card data. They had hidden a mini camera somewhere close by to catch people punching in their PIN's. Nazim was running the variety store, and Roy was running a credit card factory upstairs.

No job is finished until the paperwork is done. In Fraud, it seemed the paperwork was never done, the pile just got deeper and deeper. Norm didn't mind. He was seeing some action, getting out of the office, dealing with informants, and actually having some fun. It was really no surprise, but neither Norm or Jesse ever heard from Karl Crest again.

After every arrest, there is an interview where the accused gets a chance to confess or help out the police in consideration for a lighter sentence. Roy was willing to give up everything he knew, but he wanted something in exchange.

17
Roy Rogers

The informant information that Norm received was as complicated as the fraud investigations he was involved in. Sure, the paper trail led to the bad guys, but it always led to more and more paper. The names got more complicated too, it was the Lebanese, Romanians, Arabs, and Nigerians who were behind the fraud scams.

In Nigeria, some government officials are involved in the scams and actually encourage their people to get involved to stimulate the economy. The scams are devious and forever evolving. Some of the email spammers are relentless with their mailings telling people things like they have a family inheritance or that they've won a huge lottery in another country.

Norm worked on one case where an elderly woman got sucked into giving the scammers almost two hundred grand, all in the hopes that she could claim her sixty-million-dollar Spanish lottery windfall. Norm tried to tell the woman it was a scam before she gave all of her money away, but her greed got the best of her. The woman's daughter called Norm after her mother blew all of her life's savings. She said her mom was actually upset that she ran out of money and that she wouldn't be able to claim her lottery prize.

Virgin Territory

It was a continuing education for Norm. When he arrested the Romanian named Roy Rogers, he had nothing to say. After a night in a jail cell, he told Norm he would tell him everything that he wanted to know. The only condition was that Roy *wanted to* be deported back to Romania. It was a strange request considering that Roy had defected from there to the U.S. and then snuck across the border into Canada. He said he missed his girlfriend back home, but Norm didn't buy it, figuring there had to be a lot more to it. Regardless, he reached out to one of his Immigration contacts and put the wheels in motion.

Norm sat down in the interview room with Roy and opened his notebook. The interview rooms contain only a table and two chairs. For an interrogation, keen investigators arrange the furniture in such a way that they can openly confront a suspect while questioning them. Two of the chairs can be placed facing each other at one corner of the table, with the suspect facing the camera.

The second investigator sits at the opposite end of the table taking notes of the conversation and suspect's body language. With no table in between the investigator can move his chair closer to the suspect to apply emotional pressure by getting into their personal space. In a normal interview where a potential informant wants to supply information, the investigator can simply sit across the table from them, letting them feel more comfortable. Psychologically, the table is a safety barrier.

Roy sat there attentively on his side of the table, waiting for Norm's questions. He started with the preliminary tombstone information like his name and date of birth. That information was already in the official reports but it's an interviewing technique that helps put the subject at ease. The man sitting across from Norm was thirty years old but he looked forty-five. His name was Romanian and difficult to pronounce in English.

He said to Norm, "Everyone just calls me Roy. I always wanted to be a cowboy like Roy Rogers."

Roy was slight in stature, soft spoken, with a thick Middle Eastern accent. His head was almost completely bald, his only facial hair was his five o'clock shadow. His teeth were heavily stained from his cigarette habit. He asked Norm if could have one. Cigarettes were a great tool for police investigators, it would relax many suspects and help them to spill the beans. But the law had changed and Norm told Roy he was sorry, that there was no smoking in the building. In reality, Norm wasn't sorry, he hated sucking in second-hand smoke.

Card Players

Roy wasted no time in rambling off the names of the other guys he knew who were involved in credit card fraud. He talked about M.S.R.'s, P.M.R.'s and data chips, technical stuff that was way over Norm's head. He interjected, telling Roy he was just a dumb cop and he asked him to explain things in layman's terms. Roy spoke about two particular young guys in the city who were running illegal credit card factories from their homes. According to him, it could be easily done with a laptop computer and a few things obtained over the Internet.

The M.S.R. is simply a credit card reader, similar to the machines you see in any store, but without all the fancy buttons. It looks exactly like the machine you might see in hotels when they program your room key. The P.M.R. is a miniature version that can be easily concealed in a pocket or apron. They can be purchased online.

It was obvious to Norm that Roy was no dummy and that he knew what he was talking about. He said that he got into the business back home in Romania with a group of fraud artists. He said that most of Europe had switched to chip cards to alleviate their credit card fraud. Canada had not switched over to the new technology yet, so it was virgin territory for enterprising criminals.

Roy said that the two fraudulent card makers were named Drew and Bogart. He believed that Drew had a debit card machine set up in a local corner store somewhere and that he was skimming credit card information. He paid one of the store employees to let him run his scam. Roy said Drew had blank and stolen credit cards in his house. He didn't know the address but described the house's location to Norm. He said that Drew had a credit card embosser, but he believed that Nazim's brother Basheer was in possession of it.

According to Roy, Bogart was a young computer genius. He had started hacking computers in his early teens and was "phishing" by the time he was seventeen. Bogart copied a bank website and lured people into logging on to it with their personal data. He pumped out ten thousand emails at a time, so even if he only got three or four card numbers, it was a good day. Hackers like Bogart didn't do it for the fun of it, they did it for the money.

Roy said that Bogart had organized crime ties in Romania, where he swapped stolen credit card information. Locally, he had a buddy named Rony who was helping him to make fake identification that was used for their scams. Some of the cards that Roy got from Karl Crest went to Bogart for reprogramming. He got three hundred bucks a piece for them.

He said Rony and Bogart also had a wire scam going on, in which they were raking in thousands of dollars every week. He said they acted like little gangsters; they went to local night clubs buying cocaine and expensive bottles of champagne, while they entertained their friends.

Norm filled two pages in his notebook with details from Roy. His work was cut out for him doing follow-up for the next few days. Norm pumped Roy for all the information he had before he was shipped off to the county jail, it was difficult to talk to anyone there.

Later, Norm had to make an appointment to visit Roy at the jail to continue their conversation. A guard brought him to a tiny interview room to visit with him. Between his whispering and his thick accent, he could barely understand Roy at times. According to him, even the guard posted outside the door couldn't be trusted. He feared for his safety if anyone found out that he was a rat. His fears were not unfounded, Norm glanced out the little window at the guard and saw that he was leaning in with his ear near the crack in the door.

Roy Rogers eventually got his wish; he was deported back to his native Romania. He gave Norm his email address and said he'd stay in touch, but he never did.

18
Bazaar Brothers

While Norm was busy checking police records and chasing leads on Roy's information, Nazim Bazaar called. Norm wanted to offer him some cheese to go with all the whining he did on the phone. He went on and on about how he was just trying to run a business and keep his head above water. He had already received the team speech from Norm when he was arrested, but he talked in circles, not really saying anything worthwhile.

He gave up the same information that Roy had already given. All of Nazim's information seemed to be second hand and basically useless. He persisted though and called back on another day, saying he wanted to meet in person.

Norm always liked to arrive early when meeting an informant, it was a safety thing as much as it was a curiosity thing. Cops can get set up by their informants, so if Norm was meeting someone new while working alone, he took precautions to avoid any potential problems. He usually told his boss or one of his co-workers where he would be meeting the informant.

He learned that most informants were late for a meeting, so arriving early wasn't a problem. Norm told Nazim to meet him in the parking lot of a public park on the far west side of the city. He got there early and positioned his car so he could see Nazim, or anyone else coming into the lot.

It was only a couple minutes past the meet time, when a dark colored ghetto cruiser pulled into the lot and made its way over to Norm's car. The car's windows had dark tinting, but he could see that someone else was with Nazim in his car. He and the other guy got out of the car, they had similar Middle Eastern features, but they looked like night and day.

Nazim was impeccably dressed with tan slacks and dark brown dress shirt. His wavy jet-black hair was gelled and slicked back. He was clean shaven, but it looked like he was one of those guys who had to shave twice a day to achieve that look. Norm smelled his cheap cologne as he climbed into the back seat.

The other guy was a complete contradiction. He had the homeboy, jock-look going on. He wore brand new expensive sneakers, grey track pants and a pro basketball jersey. His hair was spiked and he had a neatly trimmed Fu Manchu moustache.

Nazim shook Norm's hand and said, "This is my brother Basheer, he can tell you what you want to know."

Basheer reached over the seat and shook Norm's hand; the smell of his sport cologne overpowered his brother's.

He said, "It's nice to meet you Norm, how can I help my brother?"

Norm was impressed that Basheer was stepping up to help his brother. Nazim either didn't understand exactly how the game was played, or he really didn't know anything. This was not the case with Basheer, he immediately dropped some of the same names that Roy did but he gave more intimate details and admitted he had dealt personally with them.

Where Nazim had a thick accent, Basheer spoke clear and precise English. Within minutes, Norm was convinced that Basheer would be able to help him take down some of the guys who were making fake credit cards.

He let Basheer finish speaking, then directed him to focus on one guy at a time. Norm still had lots of follow up to do on these fraudsters, so he told Basheer to keep in touch and see what else he could dig up on the guy named Drew. He said that he would do whatever it would take to help get his brother out of trouble.

Norm felt that Basheer was being sincere so he asked him, "As a show of good faith, how 'bout you give up that embosser that you have tucked away?"

Basheer looked a little surprised, but he cracked a smile and said, "Sure, no problem, Norm."

Dominos

Karl Crest was the first domino to fall. When he fell, he knocked over Roy, who knocked over Nazim. The dominos were all lined up waiting to fall and Norm was there waiting to catch them. He put his backlog of other fraud files on the back burner, but his boss didn't care, the Fraud Squad was getting noticed.

The brass even popped by the office to see what was going on, normally no one came by to visit. The other investigators in the squad loved the action, it gave them a chance to get out of the office and to make some overtime.

Norm's boss laughed out loud after one long overtime shift and said, "They don't know what to do upstairs, the Fraud Squad never had an overtime budget before."

While Norm was browsing computer screens and police files, Bogart's name popped up as a person of interest with the Mounties. A phone call to their financial crime's office put Norm in touch with one of their investigators. He told Norm that Bogart's father showed up at the Mountie office one day with his son's computer.

Apparently, dad had told the cops that he felt his son was up to no good. He was spending endless days and nights in his room on his computer. His son had also come into a pile of money that he didn't have a good explanation for.

The Mountie told Norm he was welcome to take the computer since he had been in possession of it for a year and never had a chance to look at it. Apparently, fraud cops everywhere are backlogged and fighting a losing battle. Norm gave the computer to one of the in-house computer technicians so he could run a special software program in an attempt to retrieve any files that might be hidden on the hard drive.

He already had rough plan on how to take down the rest of the players when Basheer called back. He created a file called *Card Players* to keep all the different names straight. Basheer had been to visit Drew and got the information that Norm needed for a search warrant at Drew's house. Drew was even kind enough to show Basheer some of his hiding places for the stolen credit cards and electronics that he had.

Search warrants changed dramatically over the years, a two-page document that previously contained a one paragraph appendix, had turned into a short novel, containing a dozen or more pages, depending on the complexity of the case. In the court's opinion, a man's home was his castle, so the cops needed abundantly clear and precise grounds as to exactly why they wanted to search the castle. The days of visiting judges at their homes disappeared with the arrival of *Telewarrants,* a process by which the process is done by fax machine.

Like everyone else, Norm missed those good old days. On one occasion during his early Drug Squad days, he had caught the judge late in the day as he was on his way out the courthouse door. As a courtesy, the cops called the judge first to tell them a search warrant was being prepared. The judge was in a hurry to go somewhere, so he told Norm to meet him at the side door.

The veteran judge looked Norm in the eye and asked, "Do you have really good information on this one?"

He replied, "Yes sir."

Norm didn't have time to fill in the appendix that was normally attached to the warrant.

The judge looked at it and said, "Don't burn me on this."

To Norm's astonishment, the judge signed the blank search warrant.

As the he hurried away, he said, "Just make sure you leave me a copy after you fill it in."

The Fraud Squad raided Drew's place and recovered a whole bunch of stuff. He had stolen and blank credit cards hidden all over in his basement apartment. He had blank bank cards that only needed the numbers embossed on the front.

Drew had a skimmer machine and a laptop to hook it up to, and electronics that he had bought with stolen credit cards. It was a good bust and Basheer had proven that he was a reliable informant. As a bonus, Norm's sixteen-hour day earned him some big overtime.

Drew had been arrested before, he immediately told Norm he wanted to help himself out and work his patch. He spit out two names like he was discarding cherry pits, Bogart and Rony. Norm wasn't sure exactly what Drew might be able to come up with to help take them down, so he told him to start digging and call when he had something substantial.

Jack of All Trades

Basheer had successfully worked his brother's patch and began collecting some extra cash as a reward for Norm's successful search warrants and arrests. He took a liking to Norm.

He came right out and asked him one day, "So what else do you want to know?"

Norm asked, "Why, what have you got?"

Basheer replied, "Cigarettes, drugs, you name it…"

Norm, always curious asked, "Who do you know selling drugs?"

Basheer grinned from ear to ear and said, "How about Fat Fiona? I play poker with her all the time."

He rambled on about Fiona and how he knew that she stashed her crack at a certain friend's apartment. He had more clout and connections than Norm was aware of, not bad for an illegal immigrant who had only been in the country for a couple of years.

Norm felt like a secretary taking dictation, scribbling pages of notes while Basheer filled him in on who was into what. He gave Basheer directions on what he needed to pursue, people like Fiona and the cigarette guys. Norm explained that Fraud was now his job, so any other information would have to be passed on, unless Basheer wanted to work directly with cops from other units.

He was content with Norm handling him and his information. Nazim showed up for the odd meeting with Basheer, but he was pretty well useless. Regardless, Norm humored him and pretended to appreciate his input.

The cigarette info was passed on to the Mounties. He went directly to his buddy Blackjack with the drug information. Blackjack was in charge of the Drug Squad, he said that Fiona managed to stay in their good graces by playing both sides of the fence, supplying mostly useless information to the Drug Squad, in the hopes of keeping them off her back. In reality, the Drug Squad always wanted to nail her, but she was a smart cookie and always one step ahead of them.

Mixed Smoke Signals

It was physically impossible for Norm to investigate everyone and everything that his informants told him about. Basheer was in deep with some Middle Eastern guys who were bringing truck loads of illegal Indian cigarettes into the city.

The loads were worth up to fifty thousand dollars each, and they were distributed among a group of variety stores across the city.

The crime didn't fall under Norm's jurisdiction, so he introduced Basheer to a Mountie investigator. He eventually helped them to take down one of the major players involved, but he told Norm that they fucked him out of his reward. There wasn't much he could do about that, so it was obvious that Basheer wouldn't be calling the Mounties back.

Norm knew Basheer was a middle man, being involved in some drug deals as well as some illegal cigarette deals. He just wasn't sure how deeply he was involved. He called Norm one day asking him to meet at a local coffee shop. Norm got to the location early as usual, so he went in for a bit of lunch.

Basheer showed up on foot about ten minutes later carrying a paper bag from a fast-food restaurant. He asked Norm for a lift home and if he could put the bag in Norm's vehicle in the mean time. Norm pointed to his grey van parked outside in the parking lot, then went to the bathroom.

Basheer told Norm that Bogart had hooked up with a new Russian guy and that another kid he had been doing the wire scams with was now selling cocaine. It was some of that nice to know information that Norm already knew; he had gotten the same from another source. Basheer could see that Norm wasn't too excited.

He leaned in closer and said, "I know where you can find a gun."

That caught Norm's attention. Basheer told him who had the gun and where it was stashed. Norm knew very well who the guy was, he was a well-known criminal whose specialty was breaking into houses and stealing high end jewelry.

They continued their conversation while they walked to the parking lot and got into the van. Norm pulled out of the lot and started heading towards Basheer's place. He was fidgeting and looking all around under the front seat.

Norm asked, "Are you looking for the seat belt?"

Basheer's face had gone white.

"No, I'm looking for the thirty grand, it was in a paper bag right here under my front seat."

"What thirty grand?"

Basheer was freaking out. He started to stammer.

"I had thirty thousand dollars in a paper bag, I put it under the seat when you were in the coffee shop."

Norm was not a guy who got excited easily, but he could feel his heart starting to pound a little faster as he pulled off the road. Both men fell silent as they frantically searched the van for the missing bag of cash.

After coming up empty handed, Norm looked at Basheer and asked, "What the fuck were you doing carrying that kind of cash?"

Basheer looked like he had just lost his whole family in a horrific car crash.

"It's part of a cigarette deal, they'll kill me if I don't deliver that cash."

Norm did what any good Sherlock would do, he returned to the scene of the crime. To his astonishment, there was an almost identical van that was parked in the spot next to his. He looked at Basheer, the color was starting to come back to his face.

"I don't know, maybe I put the bag in the wrong van?"

Norm parked down the street leaving Basheer in the van. He wasn't about to start rifling through someone else's van, so he went back into the coffee shop. There was some kind of commotion behind the counter near the kitchen, a woman with two young children was babbling away to the manager. Norm understood what had happened, but how could he explain that he was a cop and that the bag of cash belonged to his informant?

Before he could say anything, a patrol car pulled into the parking lot, the manager had called the police. The woman couldn't believe what she had found; she was afraid and didn't know what to do with the bag full of cash. Norm spoke to the cops and pointed out the similar vans. He tried to explain the situation, but officially they had to seize the cash and file a report.

Norm went back to his van to break the news to Basheer. He also called his boss at police H.Q. Poor Basheer, he wondered out loud what would happen to his daughter and pregnant girlfriend when he had to flee the country, fearing for his life.

Norm went to see his boss and then his boss's boss, to see what could be done. The word had spread by the time Norm got to the station, the general opinion was that the bag of cash was drug money and that it should be forfeited to the government coffers so it could pay for some retiring politician's pension.

Norm argued that the bag of money was actually found property and that the rightful owner has a legal claim to it, like any other found property. No matter what anyone thought, there was no proof of any kind that the money was tied to drugs or any other crime for that matter. The big boss agreed that in fact, Basheer was the rightful owner of the cash and he was entitled to claim it.

Basheer was a happy camper. The boss said the money could be returned to him, but it had to be counted in front of him, and on camera. It meant that Basheer had to go to the cop shop to get his money, but that was fine with him. He probably would have crawled over broken glass to get that cash back.

Bugs

The light at the end of the tunnel was shining brighter every day for Norm, his retirement was approaching fast. He had to try to complete his outstanding files and re-assign those that he couldn't. In Norm's job, you couldn't just walk out the door. Some of his investigations were ongoing and had been so for months. Harley Davidson and the other investigators in the office inherited some of his files.

He had to introduce the last of his informants to new handlers. Some of them weren't happy about that, but such is life. Basheer was Norm's last reliable informant; he was a proven plethora of criminal information. He reminded Norm of the guy who had a gun, a case that he had never looked into. He handed the investigation off to the detective squad and the S.W.A.T. team.

Why anyone would want to resist a bunch of guys dressed in fatigues and carrying machine guns is a mystery. Norm dropped by during the search and waited in the hallway. The screaming and yelling brought neighbors out into the hallway. He flashed his badge and told the neighbors everything was under control. The bad guy lost the fight and a hand gun was recovered during the search of his apartment.

Basheer told Norm about a local variety store that was selling drugs and illegal cigarettes. He let the Drug Squad handle that one. As it turned out, the guy was into kiddy porn too. He let the other squads handle the work, but he made sure Basheer got paid for his efforts. By sitting on the sidelines, it meant that he wouldn't have to return for court after retiring.

Basheer was well-connected. He told Norm that he had met some guys up north who showed him a shipping pallet stacked with dozens of pounds of weed. They were looking for someone to help them move the stuff.

He had another gang-affiliated guy offer him an opportunity to smuggle cocaine into the country. That guy wanted to use Basheer's girlfriend as a drug mule. The gang guy sent single girls off to an island in the Caribbean and then had them return with a special suitcase, lined with cocaine. Norm tried to get the Mounties interested, but they said it was more of an *international* case, whatever that meant.

Norm had to introduce Basheer to one of the new Drug Squad guys, he couldn't be the go between forever. Basheer told Norm and the young cop about some guys with guns, it was the fraudster Drew and his brother. His brother was connected to a terrorist organization and they were selling the guns to financially support the criminal enterprise. The young cop's jaw kept dropping while Basheer filled him in. Norm had to remind him to keep taking notes.

The last gift to Norm from Basheer was a group of hard-core B & E boys who had preyed on the city for years. He had locked some of them up years earlier when he worked in the B & E Squad. The seasoned criminals had done some time in jail, learned from their mistakes, then honed their skills. The Mobile Surveillance Unit struck out with the crew on many occasions, they were very good at evading the cops. The B & E Squad was also stymied by the crew, they knew what they were up to but couldn't figure out how to catch them.

One of Norm's buddies in the B & E Squad got excited when Norm told him how to get them. Basheer was in tight with the guys, he bought some of their high-end stolen jewelry. He told Norm the location of the store where they fenced a lot of it. The guys were serious players, the ring leader was the guy with the gun who the S.W.A.T. team had beat the shit out of.

Obviously, he wasn't deterred. Basheer said the crew knew how to pick out houses where there was high-end jewelry and electronics. One of their methods was to scope out houses with certain types of satellite dishes. They knew that specific ethnicities liked satellite service from their own countries. Some of these same people liked high-end jewelry. They kept the jewelry and sometimes large amounts of cash in their homes. The crew preyed on those people in the city, and across the county.

Basheer gave Norm a list of some property the crew had recently stolen; he bought a laptop from them to prove it. The B & E Squad confirmed the property had been stolen from a couple of houses outside the city. He asked Norm why the cops couldn't catch the crew. Norm asked the B & E Squad the same question. It was the same old story; the crew was too good and they didn't know how to catch them.

Basheer asked Norm, "Why don't you bug their cars?"

That was the million-dollar question. The crew switched cars and license plates all the time. The cops found it almost impossible to do surveillance on them even when they knew what cars they were driving.

"I can tell you what cars they have and where they're at."

Norm was impressed. Leave it up to Basheer to tell the cops how to catch the bad guys. The force had a couple tracking devices on a shelf collecting dust, so Norm suggested that they put them to use. His buddy applied for tracking warrants and Basheer supplied the types of cars and their locations. The crew had two different cars stashed in parking lots. When they went out to do a B & E, they drove to that area and then swapped vehicles. The stash vehicles were not known to the cops.

With Basheer's help, the B & E Squad bugged the cars and got lucky a couple of nights later. The tracking device allowed them to keep their distance without being detected. They followed the crew into an upscale sub-division, then sealed off the area. When the crew tried to leave the area with a car full of loot, they were taken down by the cops. They had broken into a couple of homes, stealing jewelry and electronics.

Bye Bye Basheer

Unfortunately for Basheer, he soon got to see his friends in jail. Not long after Norm retired, Basheer's new handler called. He said another Drug Squad cop had busted Basheer at his store with a substantial amount of coke and some weed. He played both sides of the fence, and he got caught. He called Norm one day whining, saying he should get credit for all the help that he gave the police. Norm reminded him that he had been paid for the information. He also told Basheer he was out of the game so he could no longer help him.

With Basheer getting busted, Nazim lost the store. It was just a front anyway, they never really sold anything legal there. Somehow, Nazim managed to get more financial backing and he opened a pizza place on the other side of town. It wasn't long before that went belly up too. Some time later, Norm ran into him managing another variety store. He was working for someone else; it is what he knew. Unlike his brother Basheer, Nazim had no problem trying to earn an honest living.

Basheer never got his Canadian citizenship, and by getting arrested, he never would. The last Norm heard, Basheer was going down for his drug bust and he would be going to jail for a while. He could have tried to skip the country, but he had two kids with his girlfriend. He was no different than many of Norm's other informants, they played the game in the hopes the cops would leave them alone. They got a false sense of security thinking they couldn't be touched, they became fearless.

Basheer was a grand master at playing the game, but in the end, even a grand master loses sometimes.

19
Rony the Geek

Drew called Norm to fill in the blanks with regards to Rony and Bogart's criminal activities. It was obvious to Norm, that Drew was withholding pertinent information and was trying to play both sides of the fence. He didn't want to go to jail, but he didn't want to rat on his friends either.

He had enough info on Rony to satisfy the judge and to get a search warrant for his house. Bogart was very careful, so it was difficult for Norm to get enough information to obtain a warrant for his place. He prepared warrants for both places anyway, hoping he could find the last piece of the puzzle for Bogart while searching Rony's place.

The Fraud Squad hit Rony's place first thing in the morning. Rony left in his car before Norm could get the warrant signed, so the cops had to follow him around until it was signed, then they arrested him. They brought Rony home and he cordially showed Norm where everything was. He handed over eleven thousand in cash, seventy fake Canadian citizenship cards, two cloned credit cards, a laminating machine and a laptop computer.

Right from the minute the Fraud Squad walked into his house, Rony said he wanted to cooperate. The cops also found a pile of wire transaction slips. Rony said he'd give Norm an inculpatory statement admitting to everything, if his wife could be left out of it. They just had got married and he didn't think she'd be too impressed.

Rony gave up Bogart, giving Norm enough to get the search warrant for his place. He just had to add a couple paragraphs to the warrant, and then they hit Bogart's place the same afternoon. His girlfriend Brittany answered the door, she was presented with the search warrant. While questioning her as to Bogart's whereabouts and checking her ID, Norm found out she was lying about her name.

That was no surprise, people had been lying to him ever since the day he was hired on the job. Her name was really Cassandra. He requested that she call Bogart, to have him come home. Cassandra was a beautiful and well-developed young lady who knew full well what Bogart was up to. He had made her fake ID so she would appear to be of the legal drinking age.

Norm spoke to Bogart on the phone. He was cocky, but he said he was coming home. During a search of his place the cops seized twenty-three hundred dollars in cash, four computers with a whack of software, an M.S.R. credit card reader, a forged U.S. passport, cloned credit cards and a pile of wire transaction slips. Norm later seized two more of Bogart's computers from a repair shop. He remained cocky, saying he had done credit cards and the wire scam in the past, but not anymore. It was all lies.

Fraud Lessons

Rony chomped at the bit to get himself out of hot water. He told Norm he would attend the cop shop to open the files on his computer that they seized. The young fraudsters were computer savvy, using passwords or hidden files.

Drew had hit a button on his computer before Norm grabbed it, shutting it down and hiding all the files. Rony kept his word and attended the Fraud office for show and tell on his laptop. He had files showing some of the work he had done with fake ID, but more importantly he had pictures of Bogart and some of the other guys who were involved in the wire scam.

Once again, Norm was amazed at how easily the young punks made loads of cash. Rony said they went online using a fake name, pretending to sell certain items, like electronics. When someone wanted to buy the item, they'd tell them to send the money by a wire transfer.

The wire service issues a code word or number to identify the person picking up the money. The buyer wires X amount of dollars to Joe Schmoe in Timbuktu for their purchase, expecting to then take delivery of the item.

The kids were ballsy enough to accept multiple buyers for the same item. Then they took their fake ID to one of a number of wire offices in the U.S. and claimed the cash. The glitch in the system is that anyone who had the proper ID and code could claim the cash anywhere in the world.

It is a lucrative scam, Rony said Bogart used him and several other buddies as pick-up guys. He figured that Bogart was making two or three thousand dollars a week. That is big money for anyone, let alone a couple of twenty-one-year-olds. Bogart never had a job; he didn't need one with the money he was making illegally.

Rony had worked in an electronics store and he had his own music business. Admittedly, he was in it for the money. He had no record and was a good kid from a good family. He was clean cut and always dressed well. Rony had a bit of a wimpy look, he was definitely a computer geek. Norm was impressed with his manners and punctuality when he said he'd call or meet up with him.

Rony the Geek stayed in touch with Bogart and reported back to Norm with anything that was going on. His case on Bogart was weak, so another arrest would sweeten the pot.

The more Norm learned; the more things appeared to be over his head. He was dealing with a whole new generation of sophisticated cyber criminals. Since the wire scam was taking place in the U.S., he had to call the Secret Service and set up a meeting with a couple of their agents.

Rony agreed to work with the Secret Service and he attended the meeting. They wanted him to continue the scam across the border, with them in tow, doing surveillance. Norm let that play out while he tried to catch up on his pile of paperwork. It was fun kicking in doors and busting the bad guys, but then it all had do be written up in triplicate.

Double Trouble

It didn't take long for Bogart to get back into business. Rony said Bogart went out and bought a new laptop right after leaving the cop shop. Norm had spoken to Bogart's father the day he was arrested. The same man, who was so concerned about his son that he brought his computer to the cops, was now complaining that the cops were picking on his son. Rony said the father changed his attitude when Bogart started giving daddy some money.

Bogart's mother wasn't impressed with the whole situation. He got himself arrested again, when his parents got into a violent domestic argument, and he got in between them. Norm had a good chuckle when he heard, but his ultimate goal was to nail Bogart for fraud again.

Rony kept Norm in the loop and said that Bogart was working with a new guy named Ramundo. He was another young Romanian, with a record for human trafficking. How many guys can brag about having a charge like that on their record?

Rony said that Ramundo was programming cards with Bogart. They were buying electronics with the cards, then selling the stuff on the street.

According to Rony, Bogart was obtaining the stolen credit card information and giving it to Ramundo, who was loading it onto blank credit cards. Rony gave Norm the name of the store and the last date and time that the Romanian boys pulled off one of their scams. He had received some of the same information by Basheer Bazaar, who said the Romanian was a serious player.

Norm made a trip to the Wallyworld store and sat down with their security guy to watch their surveillance tapes. After about an hour of recorded tape, Norm recognized Bogart as he strutted in through the front doors. He was with a guy and girl that Norm did not recognize, but the guy fit the description of Ramundo that Rony had supplied.

The store's security system was state of the art, the cameras followed Bogart right to the electronics department. Two other guys joined the group, they all chatted with each other, then Ramundo and one of the unknown guys each bought an iPod with a credit card.

Security was able to pinpoint the transactions and give Norm details on the credit card that was used. The card belonged to a woman from Italy, her card information had been stolen there and then transferred to a blank card here, courtesy of Bogart's Romanian connections.

The card should have been flagged at the checkout, but the clerk was in on the scam. He interviewed the clerk who admitted to the crime and said that Bogart had promised her a free iPod for letting the card go through. The security guy did some homework and then brought Norm evidence of another crooked clerk and even more stolen credit card numbers.

Rony told Norm that the gang had also been shopping at another Wallyworld location where they scammed two plasma TV's. Norm viewed the security tapes from that store and identified Bogart as one of the fraudsters involved, finally his greed got him caught on camera.

The Bogart files and paperwork forced Norm out of his office and into a project room across the hall. Months of investigation on Bogart and his scams was represented by boxes of files and reports. Norm spent countless hours adding up the transaction slips from the wire and credit card scams. They totaled over half of a million dollars.

Happy Birthday

About an hour before the end of Norm's shift, on the eve of his birthday, Rony called. He said that Bogart and Ramundo and some friends were all going *shopping*. The first obstacle for Norm was that they were going out in two groups to two different stores. The second obstacle for Norm was that the day shift was done, so he'd have to scramble to find enough bodies to make up two surveillance teams.

Norm's boss gave him the nod to work late. He called on his drug buddies to make up one team and some of the fraud guys to make up the other. With enough cops ready to roll, he had to get the security personnel from both Wallyworld stores on board.

Darkness fell over the city. The street lights came on and the fraudsters went out to play. Rony confirmed the game was on, so Norm put himself in as the quarterback. He put the Drug Squad spin team on Ramundo and he took Bogart with the Fraud Squad guys.

He called the play out to both spin teams as well as relaying the action to the security at both stores. They had their security cameras set up and waiting. Norm had his game on, he juggled his cell phone, the drug radio and fraud radio while he kept everyone in play. He used his knees to steer the car.

Norm knew what store Bogart was heading to, so he raced ahead and got a good spot in the parking lot. It was like listening to two hockey games at the same time, with different announcers calling out the action. Bogart had another guy in the car with him, they both entered the store.

Norm alerted the security guy who said that he had them on camera and he was recording the action. Ramundo had a guy and girl with him, they hit the other store. The security system wasn't as elaborate at the second store, but the girl assured Norm she'd be watching them from the time they entered the store.

Bogart and his buddy each bought an iPod using cloned credit cards. Norm had a hard time getting direct information from the second store, but the spin team stayed with Ramundo when he left the store. He was hoping the two cars would meet up somewhere, but that wasn't the case. He gave the order to take both cars down and arrest all the occupants for fraud.

The cops swarmed Bogart and his buddy as they went to get into their car. The iPods were seized, but the cops saw more stuff in the car. Property obtained by crime that is in plain sight can legally be seized, but a search warrant is required to search the remainder of the car.

Norm wanted to do things right, the car was impounded until a warrant could be obtained. The same thing applied to Ramundo's car. The evening's tally was five arrested, two cars impounded, three iPods recovered, and some receipts for other electronics.

When the action finally died the clock showed 2:30am, it had been an eighteen-and-a-half-hour day for Norm. He had to get some sleep so he could prepare three search warrants in the morning, on his birthday.

The next morning search warrants were executed on the two cars and Ramundo's apartment that was directly across the street from the cop shop. Ironically, from his living room, you could see right into the Fraud office across the street. During the searches the cops recovered Bogart's laptop, an M.S.R., P.M.R., and eighty fraudulent credit cards. After all was said and done, it was only a twelve-and-a-half-hour day. Norm had time to go out and grab a few birthday cocktails. He had a lot to celebrate.

A Dead End

Most people think that when a bad guy gets arrested for committing a crime, he goes to jail and that's that. Many of those people are completely shocked when they hear that the person got out on bail, even if they committed murder. It is our justice system; everyone is innocent until proven guilty.

Sometimes it takes several months, or up to two years for the case to get to trial. Unless the prosecutor can show why the accused shouldn't be released, he can get out on bail. That was the case with Bogart. Although Norm got to testify at his bail hearing, Bogart was set free pending his trial date.

According to Rony, Bogart needed some money, so he got right back into the wire scam. Wallyworld security called Norm and said they went back through their security tapes looking for other transactions by Bogart and his buddies. They found an additional eighteen occurrences. They fired three of their clerks that had facilitated the fraudulent transactions.

It was another month before Norm was able to finish loading up the five file boxes and take them over to the courthouse. He laid seventy-two charges of fraud against Bogart, mostly for local stuff since the wire scams and some stolen cards originated in other countries. He didn't expect the woman from Italy to fly to Canada to be a witness in a fraud case.

Bogart's case changed hands a few times in the prosecution office. Nobody there wanted it, or really had the time to dig into the five boxes of paperwork. Some time later, Norm returned from vacation to find out that Bogart had went to court and he plea-bargained a deal. Without consulting Norm, a young prosecutor took a guilty plea on two of the Wallyworld charges with the condition that *all* the other charges would be dropped.

That's how the wheels of justice turn. Bogart was ordered to make restitution in the amount of $1,500 to Wallyworld. He received one year of house arrest and another year of double secret probation (he was already on probation for his previous charges). That was it.

He had systematically ripped people off for hundreds of thousands of dollars and he was punished by being told to stay home where he could easily continue his criminal enterprise.

Norm was furious, it was no wonder that he drank. There was no doubt in his mind that crime paid. To rub a little salt in his wounds, Bogart's lawyer called and asked for some of his property back. Norm had to return a few things that the police weren't able to keep as part of the case. Bogart stood on the other side of the steel cage in the property room with a stupid grin on his face.

Norm tried not to acknowledge him while he contemplated how he could reach through the little window in the cage, pull Bogart through it, and pound the snot out of him. Such is the life of a crime fighter. Once again, Bogart got the last laugh.

Rony continued to work for the Secret Service for awhile but they eventually moved on to bigger and better things. Norm called the head of security for the wire company, but he really didn't care, it wasn't their money that was being stolen.

Rony called Norm from time to time with tidbits of information, he just liked to be able to help out. He had learned from his mistake and moved on. Norm last heard from Rony just before his retirement. He called to say he was a proud father, that his wife had just given birth to a baby boy. Norm jokingly asked if they were going to call him Bogart.

It was a few years after Norm retired, when he received a call from his buddy Harley Davidson.

"Did you hear about Bogart?"

"No, why?"

Harley laughed, "He committed suicide out west."

Norm started to laugh too. "You're shitting me, right?"

Harley laughed even harder. "No, he shot himself in the back of the head, then buried himself face down in a shallow grave."

Norm pictured Bogart lying there with that cocky grin on his face. It made him feel warm and fuzzy all over. He got the last laugh after all.

20
End of the Storm

"Old soldiers never die; they just fade away."
-Douglas MacArthur

As if Norm wasn't busy enough chasing fraudsters, he started getting called in to do arson investigations too. At least he had a day of rest after Drew's raid.

The boss called him in to work at one o'clock in the morning for his first solo arson investigation. Some nut bar had trashed his entire apartment, then set it on fire. The Fire Inspector had determined it was Arson before Norm got there.

Norm had seen a lot over the years, but this guy won first prize for creativity. He had torn up, smashed and broken every thing in his apartment. Dishes, furniture, everything. There was ketchup and mustard smeared all over the walls. He plugged the toilet with a towel, then pissed and shit on top of it. He put the smoke alarm in the bath tub, then covered it with a whole can of shaving cream, Q tips and cigarette butts. He cut the phone line and every other visible wire in the apartment.

When Norm interviewed the guy at the cop shop, he said he wanted the place to burn. That was the extent of his confession. He had used lighter fluid to start at least three separate fires in the apartment. Luckily, he didn't know enough to ventilate the fire and it ran out of oxygen before it could spread to the other units in the building. No one was hurt.

Norm had to get a search warrant to legally collect any evidence at the scene. That meant working through the night and all the next day. Thank God it was Friday, he had the next two days off.

A Candle in the Wind

Norm had investigated more than a few fires while assisting and training his predecessor. They say you never forget your first time, how could he, it was Christmas day when he got called in. There was an explosion at a local restaurant and foul play was suspected.

At any fire scene, it is the captain's responsibility to determine the cause of the fire. The fire department has Fire Inspectors who specialize in finding the origin and cause of fires, so the captain calls them in. If the Inspector finds that a fire is deliberately set, he calls the police Arson Investigator.

Norm threw some Christmas cookies in his pocket and said farewell to his siblings at the family gathering. Showing their sympathetic nature, they raised a glass, wished him luck, and told him they'd save him some turkey. He had never seen an explosion, but the scene was exactly what he imagined it would look like.

The building's brick walls were blown out into the surrounding neighborhood and a large part of the roof was lying on the floor. It looked more like it had been squashed, as if the jolly Green Giant had stepped on it. Miraculously, no one was injured from the flying debris. Some of the cement bricks flew right across a busy six lane road. Since it was a holiday, there wasn't much traffic. The restaurant had been closed.

Norm's boss was already on the scene, he briefed him on his arrival. He showed Norm around the field of debris, then walked him to the front of the restaurant.

"Look here, this is the best part."

There was about two feet of block wall that remained, protruding up from the ground. Just inside the wall on the floor was a red glass candle, still lit. It was exactly as the first firemen on the scene had found it. The candle was the ignition source of the fire.

The investigation showed that someone had removed the cap from the main gas line in the store and placed the lit candle at the front of the store. Natural gas is lighter than air. That means that the gas filled the upper part of the store first. When the concentrated gas settled down to the open flame of the candle...KABOOM!

The concussion from the explosion was felt up to two miles away. The force of the blast took out the hair salon next door, along with the flower shop beside that. Bricks and glass flew up to a half a block away. Even with all that damage, Norm could tell that the building was locked and secure before the explosion. The deadbolt extensions on the doors showed they were still in their locked positions.

All the broken glass was on the outside of the building. If anyone had broken a window to get in, the glass would be on the inside. Since the building was secure and the gas line cap didn't remove itself, it was a no-brainer, someone blew the place up.

As is the case with the majority of arsons, investigators have to consider the owner as a person of interest, or even a suspect. In this case, someone needed a key to get in and out of the restaurant, the owner could easily be that someone. It didn't take long for that idea to begin circulating around the crime scene.

Neighbors, customers, and employees gathered in a parking lot across the street. The rumor mill started to churn. The rest of that day and the next were spent interviewing employees and potential witnesses. The restaurant's owner was conveniently out of town and couldn't be reached.

One Lucky Bastard

The explosion was big news, the local media covered the event. Norm used the media, asking for any witnesses to the explosion. A few days later, he got a call from a guy who said he was there at the time of the explosion. He said he was reluctant to come forward earlier because he was afraid the police would think he was responsible.

The guy told Norm that he had forgotten his jacket at the restaurant the night before. He went to retrieve it, but found the shop was closed when he got there. He pulled up beside the building in the parking lot, then got out of his car and looked in the window. He said he pressed his face up against the glass to see if his coat was inside. Realizing he couldn't get in, he turned away and opened his car door.

Just as he was bending over to get in his car, the place exploded. The shock wave sent him sprawling face first across his front seat. He turned, looking over his shoulder as a giant orange fireball rolled across the top of his car. He ducked back down, trembling as chunks of debris rained down on his car.

 He managed to get the passenger door open and he ran away from his car. He was in shock. He started to freak out, thinking he might get blamed since he was the only person around. He got back in his car and drove away.

Norm hadn't said a word the whole time the guy told his story. It was incredible. Hell, it was miraculous.

He looked at the guy and exclaimed, "You have to be the luckiest bastard alive; you should go out and buy a lottery ticket."

The guy grinned sheepishly and shrugged his shoulders. Other than a few scratches and dents on his car, he had almost walked away unscathed. He said that he was having some hearing problems since the explosion.

"*No shit.*" Norm thought to himself. If the restaurant had exploded seconds earlier when the guy was looking through the window, pieces of him would have been scattered all over the neighborhood.

The owner finally contacted Norm and he was interviewed. He pretended he had no idea what happened, but he showed no signs of shock, anger, or even sorrow. His answers to the questions seemed rehearsed. Everyone knew he was having financial difficulties, but he vehemently denied that he blew up his coffee shop.

He agreed to a polygraph test, but it came back inconclusive. Even the polygraph technician agreed the owner was guilty, but the machine wouldn't back him up. The technician felt the owner had rehearsed his answers and was possibly on medication that kept him calm during the test.

There was one piece of evidence that Norm thought might hang the owner, the candle. There were no finger prints on the glass and the owner said it did not belong in the restaurant, facts that were both strange. He had no idea where the candle came from.

Norm scoured all the stores in the area and found the exact same candle in a store only a few blocks from the restaurant. The bar code confirmed that the candle had been purchased there.

He was almost giddy when the store manager told him all the check-outs were monitored and recorded on video. He brought up the video footage for the day before the explosion, but the monitor was blank. The manager thought about it for a second, then remembered that the explosion had knocked out their power and set off their alarm. The explosion also fried their computer's hard drive.

Norm interviewed the owner's wife and got the same results. Neither one of them showed any signs of emotion what so ever, it was a bit weird, they were a bit weird. Even though everyone thought the owner was guilty, and some of the evidence suggested he was guilty, it could not be proven *beyond a reasonable doubt*. That is the threshold in Canadian law.

Norm quickly learned that arson is a very difficult crime to prove. It was fairly easy to find the origin and cause of a fire and conclude that it was intentionally set. The difficulty lay in trying to connect the evidence to the person actually responsible.

Dr. Death

Whenever Norm's phone rang in the middle of the night, it was for a fire call. He was a one-man Arson Unit, so any time the fire department needed an Arson Investigator, Norm got the call. The staff sergeant in charge called him late one night, sending him to investigate a fatal fire, not too far from his home on the east side of the city.

Norm had brought the arson van home that night, so it was a short drive. He had talked his boss into letting him bring the van home. When he got called in, he had to drive all the way downtown to pick up the van and his equipment, then drive out to a fire scene. He sold the idea to his boss by pointing out that he was wasting overtime dollars driving back and forth.

The fire scene was at a senior's apartment complex. The buildings were fairly new so Norm was surprised when he arrived. The fire was already out, he was briefed by the Fire Inspector. He believed the fire had been caused by careless smoking, but there was a fatality, so the police had to be called.

There were hundreds of cigarette burns all over the furniture and floors. Norm looked around the living room and kitchen while the Inspector briefed him. Strangely, there was only minimal smoke damage. The Inspector knew exactly what Norm was thinking. He tapped him on the shoulder and pointed to the bedroom.

The bedroom was cooked and so was the poor old man in it. He was lying on his back on the edge of the bed, with his feet on the floor. It looked like he had been sitting there and fell backwards onto the bed. His pants were down around his ankles and he was burnt to a crisp. Norm couldn't help but notice the man's penis, what was left of it was sticking straight up…like a half of a hard on.

There was a garbage pail full of cigarette butts right beside the bed near the man's feet. The Fire Inspector believed a lit butt started the pail, and then the bedroom curtains on fire. The bedroom door was closed so the fire flashed through the room, but died out when it ran out of oxygen.

A metal walker was standing right in front of the victim. He had physical limitations and needed the walker to get around his apartment. While Norm was examining the body, a fireman came into the bedroom with a grappling pole and he started to poke at the ceiling right above the body.

"What the hell are you doing?"

The young fireman looked a little stunned that someone would question him.

"I'm looking for hot spots."

Norm barked back at him. "I'll call you if I see one, now get out of my crime scene. And that goes for you guys out there in the living room talking about the ball game."

He heard some grumbling as they cleared out of the apartment. A police sergeant stuck his head in the apartment door as they left.

"Hey Norm, the media is driving me crazy out here, what should I tell them?"

Norm sighed, "Tell them I'll let them know when I know."

The Forensic specialist then came into the apartment. She was a rookie in the unit, a pretty woman. She already had her camera in hand, so Norm told her to get a few shots of the apartment.

He waited for her to finish. "The victim is over here in the bedroom."

Norm led her into the bedroom. The Fire Inspector was standing near the victim taking notes. The forensic specialist took some pictures of the bedroom and the victim.

He pointed to the victim's penis and said, "Make sure you get a picture of this."

She was a bit shocked and immediately blushed.

"Why do you want me to do that?"

Norm looked her dead in the eyes and bluntly said, "That's the cause of the fire."

The Fire Inspector smirked, but the specialist just focused on the half boner and took a few pictures.

She took the bait. "And how is that?" she asked.

Norm still had his poker face on. "Well, if you look at his posture and how his pants are down around his ankles, you can see that he was sitting on the edge of the bed masturbating. It caused a spark and he set himself on fire."

The Fire Inspector burst out laughing and fumbled to catch his notebook when it almost fell into the pail of burned cigarette butts. Norm couldn't help himself and he joined in the laughter. The specialist shook her head, she was not impressed by the theory.

Norm's first fire victim became his first autopsy. Being the investigating officer, he got to attend the autopsy while the victim was dissected up at the morgue. He had dealt with many arrogant doctors before, but the coroner was courteous and helpful.

He removed the man's esophagus and showed Norm how smoke inside it could tell him whether the victim was overcome by smoke or fire when they died. He also pointed out a spot on the man's brain where there were signs of a past stroke. Norm found it all fascinating. It didn't bother him at all, it wasn't like a live victim, bleeding and screaming for help.

Norm's careless smoker was his first in a string of fire fatalities over the next few months. The Fire Inspectors started calling him Dr. Death.

The Mountie Rat

Norm got a call from a local Mountie one day. He was a drug investigator who obtained some information from a police agent, that he wanted Norm to hear. Norm grabbed Harley and sat down with the Mountie in an interview room. His retirement was just around the corner, so he was teaching Harley his job.

He had worked some fraud cases with Norm and the two of them got to be buddies on and off the job. Norm got to like sleeping in during his last year on the job, Harley was Norm's wake up call some mornings.

The Mountie told them that he was using a police agent for a drug investigation that he was in the middle of. He had a taped conversation between his agent, an arsonist, and a local business owner who wanted his business torched.

When the arsonist went to meet the owner to discuss the details, he brought along his buddy, who just happened to be working for the police as an agent. He taped the conversation. The owner's business in Motor Town wasn't doing well financially. He wanted it torched so he could collect the insurance money and get out of debt.

The owner said he wanted it done in the next two weeks while his partner was out of the country. The information was good, but problematic. The agent was only part of the meeting and wasn't going to be involved any further. Nobody knew exactly when the Arson would take place, or if it would at all.

Regardless, Norm had to report it to his superiors and let them make a decision about how to handle it. He already knew the answer, there was no way they would set up twenty-four-hour surveillance on the place for who knew how long. So that was it, submit the report and wait to see what happens.

Told ya so

Shit happens, and so it did. About two weeks later, Norm got the call. The business in Motor Town was on fire, and so were the attached buildings. It was a spectacular fire. The buildings were right across the street from a fire station, they didn't have far to go after getting out of bed. The Fire Inspector told Norm not to hurry, the fire was still roaring.

His job really didn't start until the fire was out and the scene could be examined. He had learned through experience that it didn't hurt to blend in with the crowd of onlookers. People like to talk, it is surprising, the little tidbits of information that you can pick up listening to the scuttlebutt. Like at the coffee shop explosion, where people always have their own theories. Besides, a spectacular fire is fun to watch.

Ironically, investigating arson was an interesting way to end Norm's career. He liked to play with fire as a kid and he had accidentally set the field behind his house on fire, twice. On one occasion, his mom chased him up a tree threatening to burn his fingers to teach him a lesson. He stayed in that tree all day. His buddies brought food up to him, but mom knew that he had to come down at some point.

When Norm went home his mom held his fingers over a burner on the stove until he felt the sting of the heat. The pain he felt was a lesson for sure, but it didn't curb his fascination with fire.

It was colder than a witch's teat the night of the fire. It was that damp cold that drove Norm into the fire station for a bowl of hot soup. The poor firemen froze their asses off fighting the fire across the street while Norm enjoyed a bowl of their chicken noodle soup, with his feet up, watching a news broadcast about the fire.

Harley had joined him at the scene, it was his turn to take the reins. He was the new guy, so Norm relaxed and watched the fire from the window.

There were half a dozen different businesses sharing a turn of the century building complex. All the owners were devastated, except for one. Harley and Norm already knew where to start the investigation. Because of the extensive damage, a provincial Fire Marshall was called in. He ruled the fire arson.

It was no surprise to anyone. Harley and Norm interviewed the partner who was out of town, first. Within the first five minutes of the interview, they knew the soft-spoken older man had nothing to do with the fire. He had owned the business for years and he had put his life into it. He knew there were money problems, but he'd worked through them before.

The younger partner who had contracted out the fire denied everything. The law requires that you have to advise a person of their rights when they go from a person of interest in an investigation, to a suspect. Knowing what they did going into the investigation, Harley and Norm read the young owner his legal rights. He offered to take a polygraph, but he never kept his appointment.

Norm was frustrated. It looked like another business owner was going to get away with arson, and the guy was on tape hiring someone to do the job. After consulting with the Mounties, Norm and Harley took a different approach. Their drug investigation was just wrapping up and they had the business owner tied into the arsonist in their drug case.

They arrested the men on drug conspiracy charges. Norm wanted to do the same for the arson. Maybe he couldn't prove the arson itself, but he could prove that the men conspired to commit the arson. Conspiracy is easier to prove.

It was his last kick at the cat, probably the last arrest he'd make on the job. He went at the owner hard. He had obviously talked to a lawyer. He openly admitted having a previous conversation with the arsonist asking him *about* burning his place, but he said he never *actually* asked him to do it. It was bullshit, everyone knew it.

The Mounties watched from the other side of the two-way glass, Norm and Harley had the room. Harley was running the investigation, but Norm piped up as the bad cop. He called the owner a liar and a and a coward and threw in some F-bombs to try and rattle the guy. It wasn't like television; they don't always confess at the end of the show.

The arsonist was a smart guy, he'd played the game before and wasn't about to admit to anything. The case relied on the testimony of the agent and the tape, but it was not proof of who had actually set the fire. End of story.

Fading Away

Norm had thought about retirement from the day he was hired. Granted it was a great career, but it was always just a job to him. He had seen too many guys ruined by letting *the job* consume their lives. He saw guys pass away before they could collect their first pension check.

Norm always promised himself, that would *not* be him. He considered a couple of potential job offers, but he didn't want to start another career. He took the advice of some other retirees and planned to do nothing for at least a year.

He was a single guy who loved to socialize and travel. He had done many all-inclusive vacations in the past, and some solo motorcycle trips. With having three hundred and sixty-five vacation days a year, it would be the perfect opportunity to travel some more.

Norm had a buddy living in Cambodia who extended an invitation to come and visit. It would give him a chance to see other places in Southeast Asia like Viet Nam and Thailand. So, a plan was hatched for Norm to fly half way across the world a week after his retirement.

It was hard not to look back, as he looked ahead to his future. It had been a good haul, but thirty-one years of looking at the ugly underbelly of society was enough. He had always tried to have some fun on the job, but at the same time, he gained a reputation for *getting the job done*.

Even as a supervisor, Norm never asked anyone to do something that he wasn't willing to do himself. He never did find out what Ash Kist had against him, but for the most part Norm was well-liked. He owed no one. He had worked with many partners and had made many friends over the years. In the end, he came away from the job with a handful of *true* friends.

There were too many arrests to count, but then there were those like Michael Cook who would never be brought to justice. C'est la vie. Norm locked up more than his share. He had learned over the years that justice was served better on the street, than in the legal system. The people who lived in neighborhoods like Motor Town never called the police, they always took care of their own problems.

The biggest change Norm witnessed over the years was in *people*, how many of them started caring less, showing no respect for anyone, including themselves. It was sad to see how some people treated others, including the police. He always believed in treating others, the way that he wanted to be treated. It was the recipe for his success, especially with his informants. Deep down, everyone wants to be respected.

The job paid well and the pension plan was good, so he knew he could live comfortably after retirement. He had always invested his money wisely and he started investing when he received his first police pay check. A divorce settlement stung a bit, but he was single and had no children to support.

That meant Norm could spend all his money on himself. He had the option of staying on the job another five years to boost his pension by ten percent, but he appreciated that there was more to life than work. In the end, he knew he wouldn't miss the job, it was just that, a job. He had no regrets. He surely wouldn't miss being called in to work in the middle of the night.

On Norm's last day of work, there was a coffee and cake party for him. Too bad Norm didn't drink coffee or eat cake, it was the thought that counted. He put out an open invitation to everyone for cocktails after work, that was more of his kind of party. People from the civilian, uniform, and investigative offices attended both parties. Richard Cranium and the new Chief said a few words at the coffee and cake party.

The Chief paused at the end of his speech and commented, "Norm, you don't seem too worked up or emotional about this?"

"No Chief, I've been planning this day since the day I was hired."

A parting speech is customary, he kept his short and sweet. He thanked all those who attended, and he said he would miss them. At the time, he thought he might miss the job too, but that really wasn't the case. Norm walked the gauntlet, shaking hands and giving hugs. Even his ex-wife attended the party. Norm always preferred to have friends over enemies.

The Dickhead gave Norm a copy of his personnel file that included his commendations and trivial complaints. He was also presented a picture of himself on the day that he was hired, he looked like he was twelve years old.

Unlike many former retirees, Norm still had his health, and his hair. The many years of stress only grayed his sideburns a bit. That was important to him, to be able to walk away from the job healthy, and financially sound.

The friends that he made and that he left the job with, were a bonus. It felt surreal handing in his key card, gun, and badge, but he knew that he had made the right decision when he walked out the door for the last time.

Crime, such as life, would go on, and so would Norm Strom.

The End

Rat

Acknowledgements

I'd like to acknowledge front-line police officers everywhere. Their unselfish dedication to duty played a major role in my inspiration for this book. I was proud to be among their ranks.

I'd also like to recognize the invaluable input that informants give police. They are a secret weapon in the fight against crime. Their contribution is rarely known or publicized. Many serious criminal investigations would never be successfully concluded without their input.

Finally, I'd like to thank those people who have become my fans and have encouraged me to continue with my writing.

Edmond Gagnon grew up in Windsor, Ontario, Canada. He joined the Windsor Police Service one month before his nineteenth birthday.

Ed worked the front lines the first fifteen years of his thirty-one-year policing career. The remainder was spent doing investigative work in narcotics, morality, property crimes, fraud and arson. He retired as a Detective in the Arson Unit.

Upon retirement Ed travelled extensively, writing about his adventures and misadventures around the world. His musings became a fun collection of short travel stories in his first book, **A Casual Traveler.**

The day that he retired, a co-worker commented on the number of informants Ed had. That inspired him to create his Norm Strom Crime Series with his first novel, **Rat. Bloody Friday, Torch, Finding Hope, Border City Chronicles, Trafficking Chen, Border City Chronicles – Four More, and Melaque Murder Club** follow in the series.

Edmond Gagnon has also written the spin-off, Abigail Brown Crime Series with **Moon Mask** and **The Millionaire Murders.** And he's written a paranormal thriller, **Four**. Ed continues to write and travel, and still resides in Windsor with his wife, Cathryn.

You can see all of Edmond Gagnon's books at:
www.edmondgagnon.com

Other Books by Edmond Gagnon

A Casual Traveler
Four – A Paranormal Thriller

Norm Strom Crime Series

Bloody Friday
Torch
Finding Hope
Border City Chronicles
Trafficking Chen
Border City Chronicles – Four More
Melaque Murder Club

Abigail Brown Crime Series

Moon Mask
The Millionaire Murders

Rat